wish i might

from the life of WILLA HAVISHAM

COLEEN MURTAGH PARATORE

SCHOLASTIC PRESS / NEW YORK

Library of Congress Cataloging-in-Publication Data

Paratore, Coleen, 1958–
  Wish I might : from the life of Willa Havisham / by Coleen Murtagh Paratore.— 1st ed.
      p. cm.
  Summary: For fourteen-year-old Willa, summer on Cape Cod is lonely with her boyfriend away, but she fills her time with books and working on a secret project with the half-brother who just entered her life.
  ISBN 978-0-545-09406-1 (hardcover)
  [1. Brothers and sisters — Fiction. 2. Books and reading — Fiction. 3. Taverns (Inns) — Fiction. 4. Cape Cod (Mass.) — Fiction.] I. Title.
  PZ7.P2137Mer 2010
  [Fic] — dc22

                                                          2009026315

10 9 8 7 6 5 4 3 2 1   10 11 12 13 14

Printed in the U.S.A.   23
First edition, May 2010

The text type was set in Sabon.
Book design by Lillie Mear

To my brother,
Jerry Murtagh,
fellow writer, kindred spirit.
Thank you for sharing your
multitude of gifts with me
and with the world.
Shine on, bright one.
Love you so much,
Col

Contents

1	The Sighting	1
2	Impossible Things	7
3	Postcard Perfect	12
4	Sprites and Spirits and Sea Creatures	18
5	The Bramblebriar Inn	26
6	Tina and Ruby's Beach Treasure	36
7	A House for Everyone	40
8	Willa the Warrior	44
9	American Hospitality	50
10	Off to the Vineyard	55
11	Will's Story	63
12	A Perfect Family	71
13	The Orphans	79
14	Bonfire on the Beach	88
15	The Widow's Walk	96
16	The Labyrinth	104
17	The Road Trip	115
18	Horrible, No-Good, Awful Daughter	125
19	A Book Fest	130
20	Gifts from My Father	136
21	Mum's Advice	140
22	Songs	147
23	Welcome Home	153

24 Sand Castles, Sand Castles   **158**

25 Change For Good   **162**

Willa's Summer Skinny-Punch Pix List #2   **167**

Acknowledgments   **169**

CHAPTER 1

The Sighting

I have heard the mermaids singing, each to each.
—T. S. Eliot

"It's a mermaid!" a young girl shouts, and the three of us turn to look.

I am standing on Popponesset Beach, Cape Cod, Massachusetts, with my boyfriend, JFK, who is supposed to be in Florida, *surprise*, and a mysterious new boy with a British accent who just shocked me with the startling claim that he is my *brother*. And now that this Alice-in-Wonderland moment cannot possibly get more Alice-y, a little tourist above us on the bluff is pointing frantically out at the waves, insisting she sees a mermaid. "See? See!"

I stare at the ocean, heart pounding. *A brother?* This boy is my *brother*? How can that be? My head is swirling with a hundred thousand questions, but my eyes are drawn to the water.

A mermaid? Of course not. Surely the girl saw a dolphin, a seal, the breach of a whale's tail, maybe. The wind has kicked up, the foamy waves forming shapes like clouds in the sky. With the sun in her face and the breeze making her eyes water, clearly the girl's imagination has played a trick on her. Either that or she's fibbing, a kindergarten drama queen, starlet in the making. Or maybe she simply wants attention. Who doesn't?

"Look, Mommy!" the girl shouts louder. "She's right over there!"

"Cute little bugger, isn't she?" the British boy says of the mermaid spotter.

JFK looks around me at the stranger. I can tell JFK doesn't like him.

My boyfriend's real name is Joseph Frances Kennelly. "JFK" is a nickname I use in my head. The beloved American president, JFK, John F. Kennedy, vacationed here on Cape Cod, and I like to make that connection between them. My JFK is smart and handsome like the famous JFK, and he, too, loves this fragile little peninsula jutting out bravely into the Atlantic.

"Somebody's been watching too many Disney movies," JFK says of the girl on the bluff.

"What's off with you?" the boy who claims he's my brother says, looking around me now to JFK. "You don't believe in mermaids?"

I peel my eyes away from the waves for a good look at the British boy's face. He's sixteen or seventeen maybe, tall and handsome, wind-tossed brown hair streaked blond from the sun like mine. He says he's come a long way to see me . . . that he's been observing me around town these past few weeks to decide if I was "worth meeting." *Ruff, ruff, ruff, ruff.* "Hey, boy." I reach down to pet Salty Dog's head. I'd almost forgotten he was here.

The big, old, shaggy golden retriever is poised, huffing at attention, his paws planted between my bare feet and the stranger's bare feet. Salty Dog (the orphaned dog I recently claimed at the shelter is *my dog*, although this brash British boy just moments ago insisted he is *his dog*) has stationed his golden, polar-bear-smelly self between us on the sand and is staring up at us, big brown eyes searching our faces, back and forth, back and forth, tongue dangling, *huffing, huffing* as if he's trying to decide which one of us is his true owner, not at all interested in a possible mermaid in the water.

"Willa," the British boy says.

My body jolts at the sound of my name. Our eyes meet and lock. Goose bumps pop up and down my arms despite the warm July day.

Those eyes . . . I know those eyes. I'd know them anywhere. They are the same dark blue eyes that gaze out from the photograph that's on my dresser of my birthfather, Billy Havisham, long since deceased. The same blue eyes reflect back at me when I look in the mirror each morning.

"You have your father's eyes, Willa," my mother always said, "sparkling like the sea on a sunny summer day."

Mother would often say this phrase with a begrudging tone in those years after his death, a reckless accident brought on by his own foolhardy actions. But Mother almost never says it now that she is recently and happily married to Sam Gracemore and seems to have long since forgotten her first husband.

It's as if William Frederick Havisham never existed.

Other than the photograph on my dresser and the name on my birth certificate, Willafred Havisham — "Willafred" being a cumbersome combination of William and Frederick that I refuse to answer to, as I much prefer the willa-like-a-willow-tree "Willa" — the only links I have to my father are the candy box full of love poems and letters he wrote to my mother during their whirlwind courtship, and the folder of yellowed news clippings reporting his apparent drowning in a hot-air balloon crash in the Atlantic. His body was never recovered. There is no cemetery monument.

Sparkling like the sea on a sunny summer day. My body shivers as if the salt crystals in the ocean air have suddenly turned to snowflakes.

"What's your name?" I blurt the words out to the stranger, turning my gaze back to the water.

No response.

With the wind and the little girl squealing, maybe he didn't hear me.

"Mommy, look!" the girl shouts. "Did you see her tail?"

From the sounds of the voices behind us on the bluff, the girl is attracting a fan club. I can picture the excited expressions on the people's faces as they cup their hands over their eyes and scan the water left to right and left again, hoping for a sighting. Surely they don't believe it's a mermaid, but whatever it is, they want to see it. Each wants to be the first to see it. It would be like catching a fly ball at a Red Sox game, or finding a pearl in an oyster shell, or spotting the first spark in the Fourth of July night sky.

"What's your name?" I say, louder now, still looking out at the water.

"Will," the boy from England says.

"What?" My heart beats faster. *Will, short for William.* Maybe I didn't hear him correctly. "What did you say?"

"Will," he repeats, this time clear as a foghorn.

I'm trembling now, holding my breath, ears plugging up as if I've plunged underwater.

"Will what?" I whisper.

"Will Havisham." He thrusts his hand out to shake mine. "Pleasure to meet you, sister."

I gasp and fall back on JFK for strength.

CHAPTER 2

Impossible Things

✦ ✦ ✦

"There's no use trying," [Alice] said:
"one can't believe impossible things."
"I daresay you haven't had much practice,"
said the Queen. "When I was your age, I always
did it for half-an-hour a day. Why, sometimes I've believed
as many as six impossible things before breakfast."
— Lewis Carroll

"No!" I say, my body shaking like a buoy in a storm. "That is not possible." *Will Havisham? Named after William Havisham? My father? His father, too?* No. I can't bear to look at the British boy's eyes. I stare at the water. . . . Waves waving, waving . . .

"What are you trying to pull here?" JFK demands in a loud voice. He positions me behind his body and moves toward the boy named Will as if he might strike him, as if Will is a bad guy Joseph must protect me from.

Salty Dog barks, looking from one face to another.

"It's okay, buddy," I say, petting him.

Just minutes ago, when JFK surprised me on the

beach and saw me standing here with this handsome older boy, I thought it was sort of fun that JFK jealously thought the stranger might be a threat, a summer wash-ashore wanting to move in on his girlfriend while he was away. Nothing feels funny now.

Clearly Joseph doesn't believe Will's wild claim that he is my brother.

Do I?

"It's straight-up true," Will Havisham says.

He sounds so believable, trustworthy. My brain is spinning like the twirly teacup ride at the Barnstable County Fair. *Can this possibly be happening?*

"Willa," JFK says, clutching my hand. "I'm sorry, this is crazy but I don't have much time. My dad's driving me to the airport in two hours."

JFK's words are a sturdy rope pulling me back to shore.

"I wanted to spend some time with you," JFK says with a sweet smile.

But what about this boy who claims he is my brother?

What about the mermaid?

Salty Dog whimpers and barks, looking back and forth between me and the stranger, me and the stranger. *And what about my dog?*

"Come on, pretty girl," JFK whispers to me. "My girl." His finger touches my hair and then the heart-shaped locket around my neck. The silver locket I've worn each day since he gave it to me on the night of our first fairy-tale romantic Valentine's dance in the barn at my family's inn. JFK's school picture is glued inside on one half of the heart, mine is on the other. When I snap the heart shut, we are kissing.

JFK smiles with that dimple to die for. He's so beautiful, my heart melts.

"Sure," I say, "let's go."

I turn to the boy, Will. "I'm not sure I believe you, but I think we should talk more. Can you come by my house later to talk? The Bramblebriar Inn. It's in town next to—"

"I know where you live," Will says, "but what about your mum?"

Oh, my gosh, Mother. Will is right. Of course. If what he claims is true, it would be a heart-stopping shock for her, and we are booked full with guests. July is our busiest month. I'm on duty to work later this afternoon.

"Okay, then," I say. "I'll meet you back here, say seven o'clock."

I look at my dog. I slap my leg. "Come on, Salty, let's go."

Salty Dog whines and barks at me. He whines and barks at Will. Salty looks at me. He looks at Will. Salty seems baffled. Welcome to the club.

"Why don't you meet Willa in town?" JFK says to the British boy, the icy tone of his voice conveying his suspicions. "The center green or—"

No, I think to myself. Too many people around. Someone from school will see us; with my luck the biggest gossipers, my used-to-be best friend, Tina, or my still-most-annoying friend, Ruby, will be there and start spreading rumors faster than Cape Cod fog up the coastline.

"No, Joseph. It's okay. I'd rather meet him here."

JFK stares down the British boy.

Down, down, down.

Will laughs in an offhand, friendly way, breaking the moment of tension. "Don't worry, bloke," he says to JFK. "I'll take good care of your girl while you're gone. I didn't come all this way to hurt anybody."

"Look!" The little tourist above us is shrieking again. "Don't you see her?"

I turn my gaze up to the bluff. A crowd has gathered now. A few even have binoculars. The girl who thinks she sees a mermaid is positively glowing with delight. She looks sweet, angelic, not at all like someone who would lie.

"Willa," JFK says, touching my shoulder. He shows me the time on his cell phone. His thick, wavy hair is so long now, nearly touching his collar. He says he'll cut it in Florida. It's much hotter there.

"I'll see you later, then," I say to the British boy. "Let's go, Salty."

JFK and I walk.

My dog doesn't follow.

"Come on, boy," I shout, running up the beach a bit.

Salty barks, but stays next to my possible brother.

JFK whistles. "Come on, Salty."

"Come on, boy," I shout, slapping my leg. "Let's get a treat."

Salty barks and whines pitifully, then lies down on the sand.

Oh, no. Please don't tell me I've lost my dog. I just got him! "Salty, come on, please, buddy."

"No worries, Willa," Will Havisham calls. He sounds like he feels bad about the situation. "Salty Dog's not going anywhere. He'll be here when you come back."

I call Salty one last time. He's not budging.

Will shrugs his shoulders at me, palms up in the air as if to say he's sorry, but he told me so. Salty is his dog.

From the actions of Salty, it seems that claim is true.

Now we'll just see if Will's other, more outrageous claim is true, too.

CHAPTER 3

Postcard Perfect

Summer afternoon — summer afternoon;
to me those have always been the two most
beautiful words in the English language.
— Henry James

"You don't believe him, do you?" I say to JFK as we get on our bikes to ride into town.

We're going for ice cream at Bloomin' Jean's. Somehow ice cream seems the perfect solution for this surreal summer afternoon.

"Oh, he's related to you all right," JFK says. "Same eyes, same hair. If he was younger, the two of you could pass for twins."

My pulse quickens. Oh, my gosh. This might really be true.

"I believe he's your brother," JFK says. "Maybe your father was married before he met your mother. And what if he didn't die in that crash. . . ."

"*What??*" I slam on my brakes so hard I nearly

take a header over the handlebars. "You think my father is alive?"

JFK brakes, too. He looks at me. "Oh, Willa, I'm sorry. I shouldn't have said that. I'm sure if he survived he definitely would have contacted your mother by now. It's been, what . . . fourteen years?"

"But what if he was in love with another woman," I say, my writer's mind racing, a plotline forming. "Someone in England he knew before my mother. What if he purposely tried to get away from us after the crash so—"

"Willa, stop," JFK says.

I look away. JFK turns my chin back to look at him.

"Willa. Come on. People don't purposely crash in the ocean to get out of a relationship. Think about it. You showed me the clippings. They searched the sea for days. There's no way he could have survived that accident."

"You're right," I say. "But what about Will? I wonder . . ."

"Now that dude's got a lot of explaining to do," JFK says. "What the heck is he doing here all the way from Europe? More important, what does he want from *you*?"

"What makes you think he wants something?" I say. "Maybe he really did just want to meet me like he said."

13

"I don't know." JFK shakes his head, frustrated. He checks the time again. "I wish I could help you figure this all out. I wish I didn't have to leave." He sighs and scowls, then shakes it off. "Nothing I can do about it now. Promise me you'll talk to your mom or Sam as soon as you hear his story, okay?"

"Okay," I say.

"Promise?"

"Promise."

"Good. Now come on. I'll race you."

Minutes later, we're on Main Street in Bramble, my very favorite Cape Cod town. They're all great towns, actually—Falmouth, Chatham, Brewster, Sandwich, Harwich, Dennis, Wellfleet, P'town—but Bramble is my home and so I'm Bramble biased.

JFK orders mint chocolate chip; I choose vanilla Heath bar frozen yogurt.

We eat our cones on a bench in the park, watching the tourists go by.

The streets are crowded. Our small town balloons three times bigger with vacationers in the summer months. It's a postcard-perfect sunny day. Spirits are high. People are happy. I glance at Joseph. He winks at me. My heart heaves, *Why do you have to leave?*

JFK is going to stay with his grandparents in Florida for a month. He has a summer internship with the Florida Marlins baseball team. Joseph's father is the editor of the *Cape Times* newspaper, and the head of the sports department had some connections with the Marlins. Baseball is one of JFK's great loves. That, and rap music. He's quite a good lyricist. He's quite a good boyfriend, too.

"Let's walk," JFK says, taking my hand.

We head over to Bramble Academy, where we'll be sophomores in September. The grounds are empty, closed for the summer. We walk past the track and soccer fields and up the steep, woody path to the tennis courts. It's shady and private. We knew it would be. We sit on the bleachers. He kisses me.

I start to cry. He wipes away my tears. "Hey, pretty girl," he says. "Where's that smile?"

I sniffle.

"Come on, come on . . ." he coaxes.

I manage a grin.

"There we go. Good. There's my girl."

I laugh and blow my nose. He pulls me close.

"But you'll be gone for your *birthday*," I say. JFK turns fifteen on July 7.

"I'll be back in six weeks," he says. "We can celebrate then."

"*Six weeks?* I thought you said a month." I stop. This trip is important to Joseph. *Don't be a whining girlfriend, Willa.* "I'm sorry," I say. "Have a blast. Enjoy yourself. I'll be waiting here for you. We'll still have a few weeks before school starts. Time for picnics and movies and—"

"Kissing?" he interrupts.

I laugh. "Yes. Lots of time for that."

✴   ✴   ✴

We walk back to our bikes. We hug good-bye.

"Call me, okay?" I say, trying so hard to smile. "Every day. And text me every few hours or so. And send me the lyrics you're working on. All of them. First drafts, even."

JFK bursts out laughing. "Gosh, my girlfriend is demanding for a little thing. Yes, ma'am. I'll do my best. And you . . ." The tone of his voice gets serious. "You keep your head in those books you love reading and stay away from those lifeguards while I'm gone, do you hear me?"

"Yes." I laugh. "Don't worry." I think about my friends Tina and Ruby and their obsession with the college lifeguards who come to the Cape to work each summer. Not me. I've got my boy. "I'll miss you," I say, hugging him tight.

"Miss you more," he says with a sweet, sad smile.

JFK turns to leave, then swings back again, his smile gone. "Be careful with that British kid, Willa. Brother or not, I don't trust him."

"Don't worry. I'm a big girl. Now hurry before you miss your flight."

I watch until I can't see his bike anymore. I wipe away the tears. *Get a grip, Willa. It's only six weeks. Six weeks. That's nothing. He'll be back before you know it.* I check my watch, *good.* I still have an hour before I'm due at work. My family owns the Bramblebriar Inn in town. I work a shift each day, helping out in the kitchen or serving meals. But in my free time, with JFK gone, I'll need extra provisions of my two other favorite things: books and candy.

Books and candy.

Books and candy.

All a girl needs for a summer so dandy.

That, and a boyfriend, but he'll be back soon.

CHAPTER 4

Sprites and Spirits and Sea Creatures

Full fathom five thy father lies;
Of his bones are coral made;
Those are pearls that were his eyes:
Nothing of him that doth fade
But doth suffer a sea-change
Into something rich and strange.

— Shakespeare

The little green ivy hands covering the old Bramble Library wave *welcome, Willa; welcome, Willa* as I walk up the stairs. Hopefully my friend Mrs. Saperstone is working today. She knows I'm trying to read a skinny-punch book a day for the month of July until I start my required Bramble Academy summer reading list in August.

Skinny-punch is a phrase I invented for a book that's fairly quick to read, but has a powerful impact. I want to write one of those someday.

This morning I read *Yellow Star* by Jennifer Roy. The image on the cover is striking. A young girl with old, old eyes in a fine wool coat emblazoned with the word *Jude* inside a yellow star. Jude, *Jew*. It is 1939. The girl is not even five years old when she overhears her parents talking about how unsafe it has become for Jews in Poland. The girl keeps brushing her doll's hair as she listens.

I couldn't stop reading. I was riveted.

Mrs. Saperstone is off, but Ms. Toomajian shows me the book that Mrs. Saperstone reserved for me behind the counter. *Three Cups of Tea: One Man's Journey to Change the World . . . One Child at a Time.*

"It's the young reader's edition of the *New York Times* bestseller," Ms. Toomajian explains. "You should be able to read this version in a day. It's a wonderful story, Willa. I couldn't put it down."

"Thanks so much, Ms. Toomajian," I say. "Can't wait to start!"

Next stop, candy—Sweet Bramble Books—the half-side candy store, half-side bookstore owned by my grandmother, Violet Clancy. I call her "Nana," one of the very finest people on the planet.

The bells chime a cheery greeting when I open the door.

"Hey!" a little voice shouts from below.

I look down, realizing I nearly toppled over a toddler who is sprawled on the floor sorting gummy worms into piles by color—red, yellow, green. He's got quite a collection.

The worm sorter starts to cry, and his father scoops him up.

"Oh, I'm so sorry," I say.

"You're fine," the father says, smiling. He looks at his son. "I told you, Jimmy. You've got to keep your worms in the bag."

I laugh. Good luck with that.

The store is packed with customers. I'm glad. Nana needs the business. The economy has hit some Cape stores hard. I tell Nana not to worry, though. Kids gotta have their candy. Teenagers and grown-ups, too.

My grandmother is over at the fudge case slicing up an order. Kristen and Amy, Nana's two best employees home from college for the summer, are busy at the penny candy and saltwater taffy bins. They smile and we nod hello.

Nana's face brightens when she sees me. "Willa, honey. Hi! Come give me a hug, shmug."

I want to tell my grandmother about the British boy on the beach, but she'll get all worried, and I need more information first.

Ruff, ruff, ruff, ruff, ruff. Nana's scruffy little black-and-white dog, Scamp, runs excitedly to greet me. He lies on his back, paws up, waiting for me to rub his belly. I oblige. "Hey, Scamp," I say. "How's it going?" He licks my hand. His nose is wet. I look to the window ledge for Scamp's sister, Muffles. Sure enough, there's the chunky, old, lazy, gray cat, fast asleep in her basket in the sun.

"Good news, Willa," Nana says, bagging the order and turning to me. "We finally won! I knew we would. And I have you to thank, honey. Your taffy tag sayings pushed us to number one!"

Nana's talking about winning the annual "reader's choice contest" sponsored by *Cape Cod Life* magazine. People vote for all of their "favorite things" on Cape Cod, from best restaurants to best beaches to best candy stores. Nana's been trying to win "Best Sweets on the Upper Cape" for a long time now. I came up with this idea to tie fortune cookie–like sayings onto our pieces of saltwater taffy—phrases like "Eat Taffy. Be Happy."—and I guess people liked the little bonus. It's funny how a few words strung together can make a person smile.

"Oh, Nana, that's wonderful." I hug her. "Whoo-hoo! Congratulations!"

"And we almost got best Upper Cape bookstore, too," Nana says, face all flushed. "Sandwich and Falmouth beat me again, but I'll nudge 'em out next year, just you wait. Your Dr. Swaminathan is cookin' up some super ideas to build our book business."

Dr. Swaminathan is my English teacher at Bramble Academy. He's working part-time for Nana this summer, and that's a very good thing because Nana knows her taffy, but books? Ah . . . not so much. That was her husband, my grandfather Alexander Tweed's bailiwick.

Books? That man *loved* books. Gramp lived and breathed and treasured books. He and I were kindred spirits. Every Friday I'd come here after school and he'd make us lemon tea, no milk, no sugar, and we'd sit on that old couch over there, feet propped up comfy, and "book-talk." Saying what we liked or didn't about a certain story or author.

Gramp always said I'd be an author someday. And that's just what I want to do. I miss my gramp so much. He died of a heart attack last year. Nana was devastated. Me, too.

Gramp's always with me in spirit, though. Every so often I see a red bird perched on a branch, looking straight at me, eyes to eyes, and I smile.

I love you, Gramp.

I take a brown bag from the rack and begin filling it with my current favorite saltwater taffies—peppermint, lemon, and key lime pie—then move over to get a big scoop of red gummy fish, then some chocolates and penny candies.

Tonight, after I meet Will on the beach and get to the bottom of what he's doing here, I'll go home and snuggle up in bed with this big old bag of sweets and *Three Cups of Tea* and try not to think about JFK. Stupid baseball.

"Excuse me, ma'am," says a tourist woman to my grandmother. "Can you help me?" The lady is wearing a floppy straw hat and a bright pink Cuffy's Cape Cod sweatshirt. Her face is red, sweaty, like she's just come from the beach.

"Do you have any mermaid books?" she asks.

"Children's books?" Nana says, motioning to Dr. Swaminathan, who is just passing by, to please come join this conversation. This is Dr. Swammy's turf.

"No," the woman says. "Books about Cape Cod mermaids."

Dr. Swaminathan's eyebrows rise up a notch, ever so discreetly. He is respectful and polite and would never make a customer feel foolish.

Dr. Swammy clears his throat and adjusts his turban. "I'll check the computer, miss. Follow me this way, if you please." He turns back. "Oh, Willa, I've got some skinny-punches for you."

"Good thing, Dr. S., thank you," I say. "I'll be right over."

Books about mermaids? I bet the pink-shirted lady was up on the bluff at Popponesset Beach. I wonder what that was in the water after all.

I tell Nana about the little tourist girl's crazy claim.

My grandmother nods her head up and down, smiling as she listens. "I bet the little sweetheart did see a mermaid."

"What?" No way. "Are you serious, Nana? Mermaids? You believe in mermaids?"

Jimmy of the Gummy Worms is staring up at us, wide-eyed, grinning from ear to ear, his cheeks bulging with worms and another sticky fistful poised midair, waiting to hear Nana's response.

"Of course I do, Willa. I'm Irish. You are, too, honey. Angels . . . fairies . . . leprechauns . . . mermaids . . . We see all the sprites and spirits and sea creatures."

I grip Nana's arm. I stare at her, incredulous.

"What, Willa, what?" Nana says with a shrug and a laugh. "Don't you ever see them? Please don't tell me my superserious daughter, Stella, is raising a nonbeliever."

Jimmy smiles at Nana as if she's Santa Claus. He proffers me a worm like he feels sorry for me. "Here," he says, laughing. "Take it."

"No, thanks," I say.

"Come on," he says. "Try one."

"No," I say. "I'm good."

I check my watch. I'm late for work.

"Gotta go, Nana. See ya later."

I get the skinny-punches from Dr. Swammy and head home to work.

CHAPTER 5

The Bramblebriar Inn

I was a child and she was a child,
In this kingdom by the sea;
But we loved with a love that was more than love —
I and my Annabel Lee . . .
    — Edgar Allan Poe

There's a photographer across the street from the Bramblebriar Inn. Mother said she was having new shots taken for the advertisements we run in the bride and travel magazines. The gardens are in full bloom. It's a great day for pictures.

I smile at the words on our Bramble Board:

Summertime
And the livin' is easy.
    — Gershwin

It's my job to post inspirational messages on the board. I keep a collection of quotes in a blank book my stepfather, Sam, passed on to me. Sam started the tradition of the Bramble Board. It's one of the things that makes our inn special.

The Bramblebriar is a beauty if I do say so myself. The main house is three stories high; white with green shutters; four chimneys; thirty rooms; large, wide front and side porches wrapped around; all framed with pretty trees and flowers—deep blue hydrangeas, Cape Cod's signature flowering bush, cascading pink roses, and happy Shasta daisies dancing in the breeze.

There are seven other smaller guest lodges on the property; a big, old converted barn where we host receptions and dances and other events; acres of groomed grass for croquet and badminton and boccie; Sam's amazing labyrinth walking circle; fields of wildflowers; a swing set, sliding board, and seesaw in the children's area; a pond for summer swimming and winter ice-skating; hammocks and benches; and wicker chairs and chaise lounges set casually about in relaxing spots. Birdbaths and bird feeders are everywhere. You couldn't ask for a prettier home.

The Gracemore estate was willed to Sam by his grandmother. Sam never could have afforded such a magnificent property on his schoolteacher's salary, but in her will his grandmother said that of everyone in the family Sam was the one who truly loved Cape Cod the most and therefore the estate should be his. I like that kind of reasoning.

When my mother and Sam got married, she took over the renovation of the estate. My mother, Stella, has exquisite taste in color, paints, and fabrics. She used to be one of the country's most famous wedding planners. Now her main job is running the inn, where she still gets to weave her wedding-planner magic, since the Bramblebriar is one of Cape Cod's most popular wedding venues. We hosted the wedding of Susanna Jubilee Blazer, of the millionaire Blazer Buick USA family, and the wedding of debutante Katie Caldor of the Caldor Creek chain of women's clothing stores.

When I was younger, much to my dismay, my mother wouldn't let me get involved in her wedding planning business. She didn't want my brain to get all loopy, dreaming of gowns and Prince Charmings and fairy-tale fluff. But now that I've proven myself a straight-A student with my sights set on college, the overly strict Stella has lightened up on the rules a bit.

First, Mother let me help her with two weddings, Suzie Jube Blazer's and then the wedding of our dear family friend, the former Bramble town minister, Sulamina Mum. I got to be the maid of honor in both of them! Mum and her husband, Riley, have moved to South Carolina. I miss her so much. I think it will be a long while before I see Mum, but Suzie Jube and her husband, Simon, have promised to come visit in August. Whoopee!

When Mother saw that a bit of wedding work didn't drain my brain cells, she let me handle a wedding all by myself, just last weekend.

Sam's sister, Ruthie, contacted us out of the blue to say she wanted to get married at the inn, with less than a month's warning. My mother was already booked handling the Caldor wedding, so I offered to plan Ruthie's wedding myself. And I must say, without meaning to brag, my wedding-planner debut was a success—not a glitch, hitch, or sloppy wedding gown stitch. (I sew a little secret something into the hem of each Bramblebriar bride's gown for luck.)

I set Ruthie and Spruce's simple but elegant ceremony out in Sam's backyard labyrinth and planned a delicious vegetarian dinner per the culinary preference of the bridal couple. The flowers were freshly plucked from the Bramblebriar gardens. Our assistant head chef and chief baker, Rosie, made her famous wedding cake, filled with my signature wedding charms, and my friend, Mariel Sanchez, nearly stole the bride's spotlight with her exquisite singing.

Mariel just moved here to Bramble this past year, but she and I are quickly becoming close friends. Tina

Belle has been my best friend since I moved to Cape Cod, but lately she and Ruby Sivler seem to have way more in common. Boys and being beautiful, boys and being beautiful, boys and being beautiful. Little time for anything else.

Mariel has a challenging life. She lives with her father and two younger siblings, three-year-old twins Nico and Sofia, in a crowded room at a scummy run-down motel called the Oceanview, on the outskirts of town. Mariel's mother is off pursuing a career in acting. Mr. Sanchez was injured in an accident and moves about with difficulty in a wheelchair. A town van comes to take him to work each day.

Mariel and I have very different family circumstances, but we have important things in common. We share a great love of reading and the ocean, and we are finding that we also share similar values, like we think people ought to care more about providing safe drinking water for human beings than serving designer water to pets. That was Ruby Sivler's big dilemma last month—which designer water to serve at her parents' new No Mutts About It pet spa that just opened next door to the inn. They offer filet mignon dinners, deep fur massages, and "paw-dicures" to overnight poochie guests. Mariel and I

love pets, but we rolled our eyes at the "paw-dicures."
Oh, please.

Wait until I tell Mariel about the mermaid. I've no doubt she'll believe.

Mariel once told me the sweetest story about how when she was a little girl, her mother used to say that at the end of a beach day, when the tide sweeps all the pretty sand castles out to sea, not to be sad because the mermaids are waiting for them. The mermaids sing a song and turn the castles into cakes.

Mermaid wedding cakes.

I don't believe in mermaids, but that's such a pretty thought.

Mariel also says that if you find a treasure on the beach when no one else is around, that it is a gift sent especially to you from the mermaids.

When I found Salty Dog walking alone on the beach, Mariel insisted he was for me. A gift from the mermaids, she said. I had noticed a boat harbored just offshore that day and briefly wondered if the dog belonged to the owner of the boat. I know now that it was Will Havisham's boat.

I smile, remembering the spring morning I first saw Mariel. I was on the beach early. The fog was blanket thick. I spotted something swimming out past the jetty.

It was such a chilly day I doubted it was a person, until, sure enough, Mariel popped her head out of the water and called to me.

Later, when I described the encounter to Tina, about the strange girl with the dark eyes and long ringlety hair swimming in that cold, cold water, Tina said, "Maybe she's a mermaid," and we giggled.

Inside the inn, my mother is at the registration desk checking in new guests, an attractive and well-dressed couple, locked arm in arm, in love.

"I've put you in the Walden suite," Mother says. "It's one of our nicest. I think you'll be pleased. Breakfast is on the sunporch from eight to ten. Fresh cookies and iced or hot tea from two to four. Complimentary appetizers at six, just a few minutes from now, and dinner is served from seven to nine. We'll keep you well fed at the Bramblebriar." She laughs. "I've taken the liberty of making you an eight o'clock reservation, assuming you might like some time to rest. I do hope you have a wonderful anniversary stay with us. Please let us know if there is anything we can do to make your time with us more enjoyable."

My mother should write a book about customer service. In addition to her talents as a wedding planner and innkeeper, she has her MBA. This lady knows how to run a business. She graduated top of her class, and shortly after that met Billy Havisham in a swirl of cherry blossoms in a park in Washington, D.C., and got married. *Will Havisham — is he Billy's son?* Mother looks up sharply, as if she's read my mind.

"There you are, Willa," she says disapprovingly, glancing at the clock. "Hurry and change. You're serving."

I zip up the stairs to my room. I wash my face and put on a jean skirt, pink top, and leather sandals. Running a brush through my hair, I pause to look at the blue-eyed man in the photo on my dresser. I slather on some lotion, a little mascara, blush, lip gloss, and then a squirt of perfume . . . done. Tina says she's never met a girl who gets ready faster than me. She says I do a disservice to the female species. If word gets out, all the other Bramble boyfriends will complain. Tina takes a good two hours to primp and pamper, although that girl is so gorgeous she could fall out of bed in the morning and win any beauty pageant on the planet. Tina's so pretty she glitters. I feel a pang of sadness. Are we really not best friends anymore?

Down in the kitchen, Sam hands me a tray of mini crab cakes topped with dollops of fresh salsa and tartar sauce. "How was your day, Willa?" he asks with a smile, setting some lemon wedges around the border of the tray. As hectic and hot as the kitchen is this time of day, Sam is cool as a cucumber, peaceful.

I take a deep breath and let it out. When I'm around Sam, I feel calmer. I want to tell Sam about the British boy and the mermaid and JFK leaving, but there isn't time. "Good," I say. "Thanks, Dad. How was yours?"

It stills feels awkward to say "Dad" — it's only been since Father's Day, but Sam truly feels like the father I never had, and so I wanted to give him that honor, calling him "Dad." Sam said it was the nicest gift anyone ever gave him.

"Perfect," Sam says. "Got some gardening in, planted some more butternut squash and pumpkins, scoped out plans for a new trail down by the lake. Had a nice lunch with your mother. Perfect day."

"That's nice, Dad. I'm glad." I reach for a handful of flowered cocktail napkins and head to the porch with the platter of crab cakes.

Mother is pouring a guest a glass of wine at the bar. She's wearing a striking orange dress. I'm sure there's a fancier name than *orange* for that color — *tangerine* or *sunset* or *desert sands* or something. Tina and Ruby, the fashion experts, would know. With her sleek, jet-black hair swept up in a twist and a simple strand of pearls, my mother is stunning, the prettiest woman in sight.

The guest says something to her, and my mother laughs as if this is the most delightful story she's heard all day.

"Crab cake?" I say to Mr. Pradia, a rich banker from Texas and a friend of the Blazers who is smiling across the porch at Mother. He can't seem to peel his eyes from her.

"Yes, please, princess. Thank you." Mr. Pradia takes two cakes without looking at me. Pops one into his mouth. "Hmm, hmm, hmm."

I smile. *Princess.* He calls every woman "princess," young or old, it doesn't matter. Rosie says, "That man's a royal flirt." I laugh. He seems harmless enough. And I don't have to worry about men flirting with my mother. She and Sam are crazy in love. I wonder . . . was Mother just as crazy in love with Billy Havisham? I shrug it off and move along with the tray. Sam's crab cakes are a hit.

When my shift is over, I make a quick tuna sandwich for dinner, change into shorts and sneakers, and bike back out to the beach.

It's just about seven. Time to hear Will Havisham's story.

CHAPTER 6

Tina and Ruby's Beach Treasure

*I do not know what I may appear to the world;
but to myself I seem to have been only like a boy
playing on the sea-shore, and diverting myself in
now and then finding a smoother pebble or a
prettier shell than ordinary, whilst the great ocean
of truth lay all undiscovered before me.*
—Sir Isaac Newton

A sprawling crowd is gathered on the bluff now, two police cars complete with searchlights, television cameras, and newspaper photographers. Two boys in Red Sox caps have set up a lemonade stand, smart Cape Cod entrepreneurs.

I look out at the water, nothing but waves, a black duck, some seagulls, the usual. I scan the faces in the crowd. There's JFK's mother, Mrs. Kennelly. I walk over to join her.

"Oh, hi, Willa. Good to see you," she says. "Joseph told me about the mermaid fuss on the beach, and I thought I'd come check it out."

"Did his plane take off okay?" I ask.

"Yes. He just texted me. He's already safe and sound in Florida. He says it's stifling hot." She laughs. "But I'm sure he'll have a wonderful time."

"I'm sure he will," I say. I feel a pang of jealousy. Why didn't JFK text me? I look down at the ink-blue water.

The waves are calmer now, the tide is out, all the sand castles, beach chairs, and umbrellas gone, the curtain closing on another summer day. Where's Will Havisham? Where's my dog? Will's boat is gone. I look up and down the beach. Nothing. My stomach feels queasy. Maybe JFK was right. Something's fishy. I told Will to meet me here at seven o'clock. It will be starting to get dark soon.

"Are you okay, Willa?" Mrs. Kennelly asks. "You look upset."

"I'm fine," I say, "thanks." I look over at the little mermaid spotter, her face all animated, loving the limelight. It's strange, but I think I'm sort of jealous of this child. She seems so certain about that mermaid.

"Has anyone else seen what the little girl's talking about?" I ask.

"I don't think so, Willa, no," Mrs. Kennelly replies, eyes on the water.

"You mean all these people are here based on that one little girl's story?"

"Yep," Mrs. Kennelly says, shaking her head with an embarrassed-sounding laugh. "It's far-fetched, but fun. Sort of fascinating, don't you think?"

The roar of a motor cuts though the air. I turn to look.

Will Havisham's boat is coming around the corner from the bay side of the Spit. Will is in the center at the wheel with first mate Salty Dog on his lap, *furry traitor*. My friends Tina and Ruby are flanking Will on either side, each with an arm locked through his like they've known him forever.

Tina laughs and shake-tosses her long blond mermaid hair. Ruby laughs and shake-tosses her long red mermaid hair. The prettiest girls in Bramble. A guy on the bluff whistles. He probably thinks Tina and Ruby are movie stars.

Another whistle. Somebody cheers.

Tina and Ruby wave, clearly loving the attention. They are wearing pink polka-dot Hotties bikinis — bright white teeth glistening, heads thrown back laughing. They do look like cover girls, like movie stars.

Tina spots me and waves. "Hey, Willa," she shouts, all excited and happy. "Guess who we found!"

No. How could this be happening? I haven't even had the chance to talk with Will myself, and already Tina and Ruby are involved? Ordinary people collect shells and rocks for beach treasures. Tina and Ruby collect my quite possible long-lost brother. A banner beach day for them.

A jumble of emotions, angry, embarrassed, I turn and run for my bike.

CHAPTER 7

A House for Everyone

✳ ✳ ✳

America cannot be an ostrich
with its head in the sand.

        —President Woodrow Wilson

I pump the pedals as fast as possible to get away from the beach. My head is spinning, my stomach feels sick. Leave it to Tina and Ruby to dig their perfectly manicured nails into my business. Why can't they dig for clams or crabs?

Why should I be surprised, though? Will Havisham is cute, and Tina and Ruby have absolutely world-class-quality radar when it comes to meeting cute boys. This summer they are actually making a book featuring the hottest college lifeguards in all the Cape Cod towns. They're calling it *The Beach Boys of Cape Cod*. They think it will be a bestseller. They want Nana to stock it in her store.

Now what am I going to do? I can't bear to have Tina and Ruby involved in my personal business.

They'll turn it into some dramatic soap opera episode and gossip it all over town. Mother will be devastated. And I don't even know if it's true yet.

Who can I talk to?

Mariel. She will understand.

I bike toward the Oceanview. It's getting darker, and the ride is long. Out past the cemetery, a seedy gas station, boarded-up buildings, a trailer park. I hold my breath as I cycle quickly by the refuse-recycling plant, such a disgusting smell, worst in the summer. This is the other side of Bramble, the side you won't find on a tourist map.

The Oceanview might have been a decent destination for vacationers a long, long time ago. There once was a pool, and Mariel said there's even a tangled path to the ocean back beyond the overgrown, junk-strewn woods. With paint peeling, roof shingles missing, and windows gray with grime, the Oceanview now houses very low-income people. Some are entire families just out of homeless shelters, like the Sanchezes, who cannot afford anything more than a room with two thin twin beds and a microwave.

It makes me feel so bad that Mariel's beautiful family, her soft-spoken father, the twins, Nico and Sofia, can't live someplace better. Mr. Sanchez works full-time despite his pain. He's not some live-off-the-government slouch. What's wrong with this picture, America, when good, hardworking people can't afford decent housing for their families? It makes me boiling mad when I see some of these rich transplants to Cape Cod, wash-ashores, we call them, tearing down perfectly good cottages to build gargantuan-size mansions, second or even third homes for themselves, while other people, folks who maybe grew up living on Cape all their lives, can't even afford to rent an apartment, let alone buy a house.

I sent a letter about just this thing to the *Cape Times* newspaper awhile back, and it actually made a difference. A wealthy retired couple from New Seabury, the Barretts, read my letter and announced that in celebration of their fiftieth wedding anniversary they were going to put half a million dollars into a trust fund from which a new organization called Come Home Cape Cod could draw money to build one house per year for a deserving Cape Cod family.

Hey, wait a minute. Hold everything. I wonder if they've chosen a family yet? I'm going to go talk with that Mrs. Barrett. I know a deserving Cape Cod family. The Sanchez family. Mariel would be furious if she knew, she's so proud and never wants anyone's help, but I'm sorry. I'm her friend and I'm going to help her if I can.

When I reach the Oceanview Inn, there's a taped-up sign: CLOSED FOR THE SEASON. What? That's strange.

I bike up the gravelly, dandelion-studded driveway. There are identical-looking sheets of paper posted on the doors of all the rooms. When I reach the Sanchezes', Room #5, I read the paper.

It's an eviction notice.

What? How can this be? I look in the curtainless window of Mariel's place.

Empty, completely empty. Oh, my gosh, where have they gone?

Suddenly my own worries seem grain-of-sand-size in comparison.

CHAPTER 8

Willa the Warrior

How many a man has dated a new era
in his life from the reading of a book!
— Henry David Thoreau

When I get home, I find that Mother and Sam have gone out for the evening. Too bad, I wanted to talk to Sam. He always knows what's going on in town. Maybe he's heard about the Oceanview. Mariel doesn't own a cell phone. I have no way to reach her.

I check my messages. Still no word from JFK. I text him, "Call me. I miss you. Love, Willa."

My head is spinning, thinking about Mariel's family and Will Havisham and who Tina and Ruby will tell about my business, and why hasn't Tina even called to see if I'm okay, some friend she is, but there's nothing I can do tonight. Having long since identified that I was born with a double-size dose of the "worry gene," I am consciously trying to stop worrying, worrying, worrying about things I cannot control. Willa the

Worrier is trying to change into Willa the Warrior. Worries are wasteful. Action is what counts. Tomorrow I'll see what I can do.

I take a shower, slip into bed. Opening my journal to the next blank page, I pick up my pen and write, pouring out all the stormy thoughts and confusing emotions inside.

I've been keeping a record of my life for the past few years now—the highs and lows and hopes and dreams from the life of Willa Havisham.

Sam told me that the philosopher Socrates said, "The life which is unexamined is not worth living." That's one of the quotes I've got in my quote book.

Writing helps me to learn more about myself. When I write freely and then read over my words, I see what I want . . . what I believe . . . what I love and treasure most. When I write, I always feel better.

And I always feel better when I *read*.

From the time I was a little girl, when Mother moved us from town to town out of fear of setting down roots and having her heart broken in love again, it was hard to make lasting friends. The characters in my books, like Anne of Green Gables, were my true and only friends.

Now, thankfully, I have real flesh-and-blood friends, but my favorite hobby is still reading.

Every book I read changes me a little, some more than others. Some in ways I don't even comprehend at the time, but then days, months, even years later I see a situation in a new light or act in a certain way, and realize it's because of a book I loved.

I look down at the folded-up comforter at the foot of my bed. The spot where Salty would be right now, taking a nap, or waiting, eye cocked open, staring at me, waiting for a sign that we might be going for a walk.

I sigh, my heart so sad, but there's nothing I can do.

Willa the Warrior takes action. I open *Three Cups of Tea* and my bag of candy and dive in.

Hours later, I turn the last page.

In a nutshell, this man named Greg Mortenson lost his way in the mountains of Pakistan, experienced the kindness of total strangers, and went on to dedicate his life to building schools for poor children in some of the remotest villages in the world. As I read the story I kept thinking to myself, *He's using his life.* He's using his life. *Look what this one person is doing to make a difference.*

Mr. Mortenson says there are about 110 million children in the world who don't have a chance to go to school or read a book. I look at the stack of books from Nana's store on my nightstand and then at the bookcase filled with books I personally own. I think of our large family library downstairs and the library at my school and the chock-full rooms of our town's beautiful Bramble Library. I am so lucky, so rich in books.

Mr. Mortenson talks about a program called Pennies for Peace in which groups of schoolchildren throughout our country are collecting pennies to help build schools. Here in America, a single penny isn't worth much. Even penny candy costs a nickel now. Some people throw pennies away. In certain other countries, though, a penny buys a pencil and gives a child something better to write with than a stick in the dirt.

This book says that there are enough pennies scattered about in homes in America to completely eliminate illiteracy in the world. *Imagine that.* I'll never look at a penny the same way again.

I pick my journal back up and write. *What will be your next way to serve, Willa? You helped save the Bramble Library, you led a drive to restock a hurricane-ruined school library in Louisiana, you got the inn to go green and do away with plastic bottles and such. Now what?*

I smile, thinking about what my friend Mum would

say. Sulamina Mum, you'd love her, was my very first friend in Bramble. She was the minister of our non-denominational church, Bramble United Community, "BUC," rhymes with luck, where we go every Sunday. Mum is the wisest person I've ever met. Mum would always ask me what I was going to do next. "So many ways to make a difference, little sister," she'd say, "so many ways to serve."

When the possibilities seemed too numerous, Mum would tell me to pick something I care about. Right now I care about finding Mariel and her family and making sure they have a place to live.

I add *Three Cups of Tea* to my list of recommended skinny-punch books. Thank you, Mr. Mortenson, for the inspiration. Your story has motivated me tonight. Tomorrow I'm going to put your quote up on the Bramble Board:

> Do one good deed every day and the world
> will be a better place.
> — Greg Mortenson

Then I'm going to track down Mrs. Barrett in New Seabury and tell her about Mariel's family and how they surely deserve the house her foundation is going to build this year. And then I'm going to the dollar store for three clear plastic jugs. I'll cut an opening in each lid, mark the jugs CHANGE FOR GOOD, and put one on my dresser, one on Mom's, and one on Sam's. At night, when we empty our pockets, we'll have a convenient place to dump our coins. I bet Nana will want a jug, too, and maybe Mrs. Saperstone and . . .

I yawn, tired. Yikes, what a day. I check my messages. Still no JFK. I text him again and wait for a reply. I put my phone by my pillow so I'll be sure to hear when he responds. *Have you forgotten me already?*

I close my eyes.

Soon today's recap of my life movie begins playing in my mind: Will Havisham's startling claim, Salty Dog's betrayal, the little tourist girl on the bluff, kissing JFK good-bye, Jimmy of the Gummy Worms, Tina and Ruby waving from the boat, the eviction notice at the Oceanview Inn. *Where are you, Mariel?*

And what was that in the ocean today? Just what did that little girl see?

CHAPTER 9

American Hospitality

✴ ✴ ✴

Little drops of water,
Little drops of sand,
Make the mighty ocean
And the pleasant land.

— Julia Fletcher Carney

I didn't sleep well at all last night, but I wake to the aroma of something delicious baking downstairs. Rosie is making the breakfast sweet treats—scones and breads and muffins—and that puts a smile on my face.

I check the clock. Five A.M. I might still catch the sunrise.

I throw on some clothes, head downstairs, lift my bike from the rack, and I'm off. This morning, I head to Sandy Beach. That way I can walk up to Popponesset, a good mile or so beach walk, and end out on the Spit, where Will's boat should be. It's way too early for Tina and Ruby to be nosing about. They don't get up until noon. They need their beauty sleep.

It's cool this morning, refreshing. I take a good, deep breath in. The sky is a gorgeous salmon color with ribbons of pink and purple.

When I reach the beach stairs, I scan the horizon and lucky me, *thank you*, just this very moment the sun is rising out of the blue. A brand-new day. That small fireball is rising at a fast clip, as if some netherworld creature gave it a good toss-up this morning.

Netherworld creature? I laugh. *Oh, Willa, you are so dramatic.* Where did that come from? Too much thinking about mermaids, that's where.

"Mermaids," I say aloud. "Give me a break."

Giggling. Someone is giggling.

I turn and look around me, up and down the beach.

I'm alone. No one in sight.

I walk faster. *Silly Willa, your mind's playing tricks on you.*

Giggling.

There it is again. I stop and swirl around. I could swear I hear giggling. Maybe it's that little tourist girl, the mermaid spotter, hiding so I won't see her.

Splat, swoosh, splash. Sounds out in the water now. I turn and look. Nothing.

Giggling. I swing back to the beach.

Splash. I look to the sea. A few droplets of water spray across my face.

I shiver. This is crazy. I set off at a run.

✹　　✹　　✹

After a bit, I see there are people up ahead of me on the beach. As I get closer and realize who they are, I don't know whether to laugh or cry.

You've got to be kidding me.

My possible brother Will is sitting cross-legged in the center of the pretty pink poshy quilt I recognize from Tina's princess bedroom. Salty Dog is sitting next to the king, chowing down on something tasty, probably a designer dog treat from Ruby's No Mutts About It. Furry traitor.

Tina is sitting on one side of Will. She takes something out of a beach pack, unwraps it, and hands it to Will. A fried-egg sandwich, it looks like.

Ruby is sitting on Will's other side. She lifts what looks like a muffin out of a magazine-perfect old-fashioned wicker picnic basket, and when Will's done chewing a bite of his sandwich, she offers him some.

Will is smiling like the Cheshire Cat from *Alice in Wonderland*—no, better yet, that comic-strip Garfield cat, happiest when he's eating.

Salty Dog looks up and sees me. He lowers his big

brown eyes shamefully and turns back to his treat. My heart sinks.

"What are you doing here?" I demand, looking at Tina and then at Ruby.

"Oh, hi, Willa," Tina says. "Gosh, you scared me, sneaking up on us like a ghost. I made breakfast for your brother."

"Me, too," Ruby says. "I baked."

I sneer at Ruby like she's that slimy black stuff you devein from a shrimp. "Since when do you bake, Ruby?"

"Since this morning," Ruby says, smiling, all rosy-cheeked apple-pie innocent. "Somebody needs to show this sweet British boy some American hospitality. You ran off and left him all alone last night."

I stand there sputtering like a fish caught on a line. There's so much I want to say but I'm afraid I'll scream or cry or pull someone's mermaid hair out. "I'll talk to you later," I say to Will.

"Sure," he says. "I'll be here."

Salty Dog whimpers, but stays.

"Traitor," I mumble under my breath, and turn to leave.

"Willa, wait," Tina says, standing, her former-best-friend guilt finally surfacing. "Want some breakfast?"

"No, thanks. I've got to go to work."

"Oh, that's too bad," Ruby says, feigning sincerity. Her family's so rich; she'll never have to work. "It's such a nice day."

"Shut up, Ruby," I snap.

"Uh-oh," Will says. He laughs, eyebrows raised, surprised at me.

"You, too," I say to him, and storm off.

I hate when people laugh at me.

CHAPTER 10

Off to the Vineyard

✴ ✴ ✴

The fair breeze blew, the white foam flew,
The furrow followed free;
We were the first that ever burst
Into that silent sea.

— Samuel Taylor Coleridge

Rosie is on kitchen duty when I get back to the inn. Rosie is in her early twenties. Thin, pretty, a single mom. An unbelievably talented baker. I keep telling her she should write cookbooks and have her own television show. My mother gets mad when I say these things because she doesn't want to lose Rosie as an employee.

"Good morning, Willa," Rosie shouts over the bustle of the busy kitchen.

"Morning, Rosie," I say without much enthusiasm.

"Rough night?" Rosie asks, coming over next to me, drying her hands on a towel.

"Yeah, sort of," I say.

"Here, sit and have breakfast," she says. "You'll feel better."

Rosie puts a gigantic muffin, steam rising, still warm from the oven, on a plate. She pours me a glass of orange juice. "And I'll make you some tea. You've got time."

"You don't have to wait on me, Rosie. You've got plenty to do."

"It's my pleasure," Rosie says. "I'm happy to."

The muffin smells divine. My mouth waters as I spread a bit of butter across the top. Rosie is so talented with breads and pies and cookies, pretty much anything you make in an oven, but her pièce de résistance is cake.

Our friend, Chickles Blazer, Suzanna's mother, was so impressed with the cake Rosie baked for her daughter Suzanna's wedding that she said she was going to "make her famous." I noticed Rosie got a letter with a return address from Mrs. Blazer last month. Rosie hasn't mentioned anything. I wonder what's up.

I take a bite. *Pop-pop-pop* . . . sweet and tart berry flavors explode like fireworks in my mouth. "Oh, my gosh, Rosie, this is delicious. How many different berries are in here?" I swallow and take another bite, have a sip of juice. What a lucky duck I am to have food like this every day.

"Let's see," Rosie says, "raspberries, blueberries, strawberries. Vanilla almond cake batter. I thought it would make a nice red, white, and blue theme for the holiday."

"Oh, that's right. Tomorrow's the Fourth of July."

"You don't seem excited," Rosie says.

I think about JFK, how we would have watched the fireworks somewhere together. Why hasn't he called me? "I'm sure I'll do something with my friends," I say. Tina said that Ruby and the other Bramble Burner cheerleaders are planning a bonfire on the beach. A bunch of girls from school—Caroline, Lauren, Emily, Shefali, and Chandler—are bringing food. Our friends Luke and Jessie might get their band, The Buoy Boys, to play. At the very least there will be boom boxes, and everyone will end up dancing; budding bestselling authors Tina and Ruby will dance with college lifeguards if they get their holiday wish.

I picture Tina and Ruby serving Will breakfast on the beach. They're probably inviting him to the bonfire right this moment. Once that happens, everyone from school will know. I'm going to have to tell Mother about Will. My stomach clenches. I put the muffin down. I need to talk to Mariel. Or JFK. Oh, I wish he were here.

"What about you and Liliana?" I say. That's Rosie's little daughter. "What are you doing for the holiday?"

"My friend Tara invited us over for a barbecue, then we'll go somewhere to watch the fireworks, I'm sure. Last year, Lilly was a baby. All that noise scared her. But this year, I think she'll have a blast."

I pick up the *Bramble Record* and scan the headlines. There's an article about the town closing down three motels known for housing guests for more than the legally permitted thirty days at a time. The Oceanview was one of the places they closed. A man in the story is quoted saying the town ought to figure out where these people are going to stay. "Renting a motel room was all they could afford," he said. "Now where are they going to live?"

Exactly. My heart pounds. I can't wait to talk with Sam after work.

"Thanks for breakfast, Rosie!" I wash my hands, put on an apron, grab a decanter of fresh-brewed coffee in one hand, decaf in the other, and make my way to the sunporch.

I circulate among the tables, offering refills to our guests, making pleasant inquiries as to their plans for the day or where they went last night. The anniversary couple, Mr. and Mrs. Baker, are heading out on a whale watch. Mr. Pradia enjoyed a Cape Cod league baseball game last night. The Hyannis Mets won. A group of friends, four really fun ladies from New York, here celebrating the one named Ellen's fortieth birthday, the "Ya-Ya's" they call themselves, are still laughing about the great time they had out at the Beachcomber in Wellfleet last night.

"I haven't danced like that since high school," Ellen says, laughing.

"I *never* danced like that," another one says. "That band was great!"

Later, I clear the tables, load the dishwasher, and then head out to the vegetable garden to look for Sam.

Sam doesn't know much more about the situation at the Oceanview than was reported in the paper, except for one very interesting fact. Last night, he and my mother ran into Ruby Sivler's parents at the movies in Mashpee Commons. It seems Mr. Sivler, a real estate developer, has plans for a new upscale condominium complex on the outskirts of town.

"He said he'd be interested in buying the Oceanview property if it ever became available." Sam purses his lips and rubs his chin. "This eviction would certainly speed up the process for him if the place goes on the market."

"I bet Mr. Sivler's the one who blew the whistle," I say. "That crook probably caused the eviction. He's such a slimy fish."

"Now, Willa," Sam says, always the fair-minded, innocent-until-proven-otherwise sort. "You don't know that to be true. Let's not—"

"I know, Dad. I know. But what about Mariel's family? What are they going to do? Where do you think they've gone?"

"I'm not sure, Willa, but my guess would be relatives or—"

"They don't have family around here."

"A homeless shelter?" Sam suggests.

"But the nearest one is in Hyannis," I say.

"Or possibly the Red Cross or a church they were affiliated with."

"Wait a minute, Dad. I just remembered. JFK's mother, Mrs. Kennelly, knows the Sanchez family. She was the one who encouraged them to come to Bramble in the first place. Maybe she has some information."

✳   ✳   ✳

When I get to the Kennellys', no one is home. I wish I had paper and a pen to leave a note. I'll try back later. I head to Popponesset Beach.

It's a beautiful day. I see the mermaid spotter with her mother, back on the watch again, this time with a smaller fan club. The beach is packed with picnickers, sunbathers, colorful striped beach umbrellas. Out on the water there are sailboats, kayaks, floats of every shape and size.

A bronzed and buff college lifeguard surveys his kingdom from his wind-weathered wooden throne. My gaze rests on a mother and two little girls decorating a very fancy sand castle, shaped like a wedding cake, three tiers high with shells and loopy strands of seaweed frosting.

"Willa!"

That's Will's voice. I search the crowd for his face and then I see him waving to me. Thankfully, no Tina or Ruby. I go to him.

"I'm sorry about this morning," he says with a sheepish smile. "Your friends have powerful powers of persuasion. Talk about flirts. And I thought British girls were bad." He laughs. "Forgive me?"

"Nothing to forgive," I say. "You don't owe me anything."

"Oh, yes, I do," he says. "I owe you an explanation. Take a ride on my boat with me, will you? My chum from boarding school's family has a house over on the Vineyard. It's a short ride. I'll have you back in a few hours."

The island of Martha's Vineyard. It's about a twenty-minute ride, I think. I look at his motorboat. It seems safe and sturdy enough. Thankfully, it's not a sailboat. I don't do well with little boats on the ocean, but that's a different story.

I look at Will's face. He smiles reassuringly. He's awfully charming. JFK doesn't trust him. Do I?

A seagull squawks, the lifeguard blows his whistle, a breeze sends ripples of foam across the waves. I close my eyes for a second to focus inward and take a Willa-reading of my feelings.

"Okay," I say. "Let's go."

CHAPTER 11

Will's Story

A man may stand there [Cape Cod]
and put all America behind him.
— Henry David Thoreau

With the roar of the motor making conversation nearly impossible, Will and I ride out to the Vineyard in silence.

When we approach the harbor, which is bustling with tourists, Will cuts the engine.

"Gosh, you drive fast," I say, my hair a windblown bird's nest.

"You should see me in my car back home," he says with a laugh.

I wonder about Will's home "across the pond." I've always wanted to visit England, birthplace of Shakespeare and Dickens and so many literary heroes.

Will maneuvers the boat skillfully, past one of the large ferries from Hyannis and numerous smaller yachts and motorboats, into an open spot.

"There you are," a dockhand says to Will. "The Southends have been asking about you."

"The Southends?" I ask.

"Chauncey Southends," Will says as he ties up the boat. "My chum from Bainbridge's family. I'm staying with them for a while."

"Bainbridge is your boarding school?"

Will nods. "Come on. I know a place where we can talk."

We head into town, past the busy shops and restaurants and out onto a quaint, quieter street lined with stately historic homes. When we turn a corner, Will stops in front of a bakery. "Let's get a sweet," he says.

Will pays for two oatmeal raisin cookies and iced coffees to go. "Come on this way," he says. I follow him up a path and through a wooded area. Eventually we come out into a clearing. We are facing an old cemetery.

"Wait till you see this place," Will says.

The graveyard looks like it's been here since the Pilgrims landed; probably some are even buried here. The etched names and dates on the headstones are faded with age and weather. Many of the markers are crumbling, most are moss covered. The place could feel dreary except for the flowers. There are colorful wildflowers everywhere. Queen Anne's lace and daisies, thistles and brown-eyed Susans. I smile. It's pretty here, tranquil. Sam would like this place.

I find myself saying the names on the gravestones in my head as we pass. Smith. Barnes. Rockwell. Spaulding. Morrow. Fletcher. Hunt. Some simply say MOTHER or FATHER. *What were their names?* I wonder.

Will sits on a marble bench. I join him. I munch on the cookie, take a sip of coffee, steal a side-glance at his face.

He looks nervous. Why should he be nervous? It's me who should be nervous. My whole life may be about to change.

"Just blurt it out," I say.

Will laughs, a big, long, satisfying laugh.

"What's so funny?" I say.

"You," he says. "You're a plucky one. I knew you'd be. From all those stories about your famous mum on the Internet, I had a feeling she was a tad too tightly strung, a bit too full of herself. But you? Nah. When I read that newspaper story about how you saved that old library, I thought—"

"You read about that?" I say. "All the way over in England?"

Will bursts out laughing again. "Welcome to the World Wide Web, sister."

My heart skips at the word *sister.*

"Haven't you ever done a search of your name online?" Will says.

"No," I say. "It never occurred to me."

"Well, try it when you get home," he says. "You're making quite a name for yourself, taking on causes like Princess Diana or Mother Teresa, standing up on your little soapbox spouting your opinions and dashing off letters to the editor like you're the prime minister himself. You'd love Speaker's Corner in London."

"What's wrong with having opinions?" I say, standing up.

"Not a pitty thing," Will says. "I think it's adorable."

Ugh. I hate that word, *adorable*.

"All right," I say. "Enough about my life. Tell me exactly who you are and what you're doing here."

"Straight out, then," Will says. "I like that."

My heart is pounding. *Careful what you ask for, Willa.*

"Sit down," Will says. I do.

He stands up. "Okay, then." He clears his throat. "How much do you know about your father, Billy Havisham?"

"Not much," I say. "Just that he died in a hot-air balloon crash the day after he and my mother were married. It turned out I was a wedding-night baby. He never even knew I existed."

"That's funny," Will says. "He never knew about me, either."

"Tell me," I say.

"Okay, well, about three years or so before your mother married Billy Havisham, he had been in love with another woman, my mum, Annie Bolton. She was the only daughter of the Kensington Boltons, maybe you've heard of them. They're one of the richest families in the UK, bigwigs, banks and Thoroughbred horses mostly. Her parents, my grandparents—hopefully you'll never have to meet them—they're a wicked cold lot, those two, they hated Billy Havisham. They thought he was an irresponsible, reckless, foolish American, not good enough for Bolton blood. Any man trying to make a living writing little advertising ditties and jingles couldn't possibly be good enough for their daughter."

"He ran an advertising agency," I say, remembering one of the few things Nana told me about my birth-father. My mother always refused to talk about him. "His company was called 'What's the Big Idea?'"

Will nods. "Clever title."

"Yes," I say. "I guess he had quite a way with words."

"Back to the story," Will says. "My grandparents had my mum pegged to marry another bloke, Russell Denwood, of the Denwood furniture fortune. My mother was a weak bird and couldn't defy her parents. She spent her whole life trying to please them and couldn't change course then. She broke it off with Billy Havisham, broke his heart, she said, and he left London the following day. Shortly after, my mum realized she was carrying Billy's baby."

"You?" I say.

Will nods. "Pleasure to meet you," he says.

We're silent for a minute. *So it's true. We had the same father. Will is my brother. I have a brother. Wow.*

A red bird flits by and perches on a headstone. A breeze cools my face.

"So did your mother marry that Denwood guy?" I ask.

"No," Will says, shaking his head. "When the Denwoods discovered my mum was pregnant with another man's child, they called the whole thing off. They threatened to disinherit their son, take away every penny, if he married 'that tramp,' as they called her. Denwood, the wormy bloke, wasn't about to give up his inheritance. My mother slunk off to live with her aunt Clarissa who had a sheep farm out in Wiltshire. That's where I was born."

My head is spinning, trying to take in this story as it unfolds, here in this old cemetery. The red bird is staring at me. "So do you still live on that farm?"

"No." Will shakes his head sadly. "My mum passed on when I was little. My grandparents galloped in and swooped me up from the sheep farm like the trophy at a foxhunt and brought me to their estate to live. They thought I'd be an interesting diversion, sort of like a puppy or—"

"Oh, my gosh," I interrupt. "I'm sorry, but that reminds me. Where's Salty Dog?"

"No worries," Will says. "Your friend Ruby took Salty for—let's see, what did she say—oh, right. A day of pampering at her poochie spa."

"Oh, great," I say, rolling my eyes. "Never mind. Go on."

Will laughs. "Well, my grandparents are rich as royalty, thirteen servants, grand manor estate, land the size of London. You Americans would probably say it's a castle. Not to me. To me it was a prison, Tower of London. I couldn't wait till they shipped me to boarding school. Least now I've got people to talk to."

"I'm sorry to hear about your mother," I say.

"Thanks," Will says. "She was a weak one, but she loved me."

"I'm curious," I say. "Why didn't you just write to

me if you wanted to make a connection? Wasn't it a bit extreme to boat over to the Cape and . . ."

I stop talking when I see how Will is staring at me. There's something more. Something he's not telling me. "What?" I say. "Come on."

"No," he says, "that's all." Will watches a squirrel climbing a headstone. He tosses the squirrel a cookie crumb. I look over. The red bird is still there.

"No," I say. "Tell me the rest."

"That's enough for today," Will says, standing up.

"Tell me, Will. Now."

Will sips his iced coffee all the way down to the gurgle-slurp, his eyes never leaving mine. He sighs. "Okay," he says, "here goes."

My heart is pounding like storm waves against the jetty.

Will hesitates.

"What? What?" I say. "Straight out with it. Now."

"I think our father is still alive, Willa. I think he's somewhere on Cape Cod."

CHAPTER 12

A Perfect Family

✴ ✴ ✴

The sun was shining on the sea,
Shining with all his might:
He did his very best to make
The billows smooth and bright —
And this was odd, because it was
The middle of the night.
                    —Lewis Carroll

Good thing for the roar of the motor so I don't have to talk as Will rides us back across Nantucket Sound to Popponesset Beach. The sky is clouding up now, the water choppy. A large sailboat zips past us, sails puffed full of wind. I think of my disastrous date with JFK last month when he surprised me with a ride on his little Sunfish sailboat. How silly I was to be scared.

Suddenly all of my previous fears and worries seem minnow-fish foolish.

What if Will's theory is true? What if my father is still alive?

It's chilly. I shiver, wrapping my arms around my chest.

Will notices and offers me a jacket.

"Thanks," I say. I take the jacket, zip it up. I zip my lips, too. I move to sit as far away from him as I can, eyes squeezed tight against the wind.

My birthfather, Billy Havisham, might be alive? He might be somewhere here on Cape Cod? I'm barely over the shock that I have a brother I never knew I had, and now this mind-numbing possibility that I might have a father, too? And, oh, my gosh, how will Mother react?

The theories Will shared with me just now in that Vineyard cemetery are filled with Swiss cheese holes. His evidence, if you could call it that, is flimsy slim, old newspaper photos and hunches. Either this is a very cruel joke or he is delusional. Or maybe, just maybe, he's right.

No. No. No. I shake my head against the wind.

Finally, my mother is happy. I am happy. For the first time in my life, I can call a place "home." At last my mother has stopped making us move like nomads. We've set down roots. We have a nice house. Good friends. Nana and Sam. Wonderful Sam. The man who has been a real father to me. The man I now call "Dad."

It took my mother more than a decade to get over

the pain of Billy Havisham's death. She dove into her work with an all-consuming force, refusing to fall in love again, frozen like a statue in a cathedral. I tried for years to match her up with nice men, potential fathers for me—*oh, how I wanted a father, a real father*—but no, Mother refused to crack.

Then along came Sam. A soft-spoken English teacher, a poet, a man who designed and built a spiritual circle, a labyrinth rimmed with flowers, a man who never has a harsh word to say about anyone, a man who fills bird feeders and plants butternut squash. Sam, wonderful Sam. With quiet patience and persistence he loved Stella with a love as powerful as the Crusades, and wouldn't let my mother run away again.

Finally, I have a perfect family. And now, after all these years, now there's a chance that my birthfather is still alive? NO. It can't possibly be true. . . .

"Willa," Will shouts, snapping me out of my reverie. "See that over there?" He cuts the motor abruptly. The boat rocks in the wake. I quickly grip the side for support.

"What are you doing?" I say, annoyed.

"Look," he shouts all excitedly. "There it is again!" He laughs. "I saw a tail flip up over—"

"Stop," I say, cutting him off before he starts any more baloney-talk about mermaids. "We're out in the middle of the Atlantic Ocean. There are thousands of fish. They all have tails. Dolphins, seals, whales. So what if—"

"I know what a whale's tale looks like, Willa," he says, sounding like I've truly hurt his feelings. "This was different."

"That's enough, Will. I'm done. Take me back right now," I say. "I've had enough of your stories for one day."

"But, Willa . . ."

"But nothing. I don't believe in mermaids. I'm not sure I believe in you. Take me home. Now."

When we get back to Popponesset Beach, there are only a few people still standing with the little girl on the bluff. The police cars and television station vans are gone.

"I'm sorry for snapping," I say to Will. "I need time to think."

"Sure, I understand," he says. "I'll be tied up with the Southends tomorrow for the holiday, anyway. Here's my number." He hands me a slip of paper. "Call me when you want to."

I stuff the paper in my pocket and hurry up the beach stairs.

As I pass the little mermaid spotter, I hear her mother say, "I'm sorry, Natalie, but it's time to go. We still have to pack up and clean the cottage."

Their vacation rental time must be up, another family moving in tomorrow.

"No, Mommy, please," the little girl begs. "She'll come back. I know she will."

"I'm sorry, Nat, really, honey, but we can't stay here any longer. Daddy will be worried. Our vacation's almost over. Let's not spoil it, okay? We'll be back next summer. You'll have another chance then."

The girl is crying. I feel sorry for her. She'll have to wait a whole year to enjoy this place again. I remember looking forward to that week or two each summer when I would come to visit Nana. Now, I am so lucky to live here all year-round.

Billy Havisham might still be alive? How will Mother react? What if she freaks out and says we have to move again? I want to tell her, but I am afraid. Should I tell Sam? No. That seems like such a betrayal to tell Sam before Mother. Billy Havisham was her husband. Oh, my gosh, I'm so confused.

Home at the Bramblebriar, I hurry past guests relaxing on the porch. I'm not in the mood for happy chatter.

I want to be alone. I notice a poster for the annual Sand Castle Competition at South Cape Beach this Saturday. I sneak past Mother, busy on the phone at the registration desk. If she sees me she'll know something is wrong. She reads my face like a calculator, never missing a thing.

I tell Makita, one of our workers, that I've got a headache and would she please tell my mother that I'm going to bed early. Upstairs, I check my cell phone. Still no JFK. *Where are you?* No "miss you, pretty girl" or "I hate Florida without you" or "wish you were here" or "I'm flying home early . . . baseball is a bore." I plop on my bed and stare at the ceiling.

A few minutes later there's a soft knock at the door.

It's Rosie with a tray of soup and some crackers.

"I'm leaving for the day," Rosie says. "Makita said you weren't feeling well. Just thought I'd bring this in case you got an appetite."

"Thanks, Rosie," I say, turning my face toward the wall.

She comes over to my bed and strokes my hair. "Are you okay?"

Her kind voice brings tears to my eyes. Maybe I can tell her. . . . No. She's been working all day and I'm sure she's tired and anxious to get home to Lilly. That would be selfish of me. I turn to her and feign a smile. "Just missing my boyfriend," I say.

"Oh, of course. I should have known," Rosie says, laughing. "Hang in there, girl, it's only a few weeks. He'll be back before you know it."

When Rosie leaves, I open my journal and write so long and hard my hand cramps up. I eat the now-cold chicken soup, grateful I don't have to face my mother downstairs. I try calling JFK. No answer. I leave him a text message. "It's true. Will is my half brother. I need to talk to you. Please call. Willa."

Reading will take my mind off things.

I leaf through the stack of skinny-punch books Dr. Swammy selected for me. The nice part about having a bookstore in the family is that I get my choice of paperbacks free of charge. That's good because I like to read with a pen in my hand, marking up things that move me.

I open *Song of the Trees* by Mildred D. Taylor. It's only fifty-two pages long. The main character, Cassie, loves the big old trees in the forest by her house. She talks to them and they sing to her. Others try to tell her that trees can't sing, it's just the wind, but Cassie knows better than that.

I think of the little mermaid spotter, back at her rented cottage packing to go home. I bet when she leaves the Cape tomorrow, as her family's car is crossing over the Bourne Bridge to the mainland, she'll be taking one good last look down at the water in the Cape Cod Canal, earnestly hoping for one final glimpse of that mermaid she knows for certain appeared to her, even if nobody else believes.

✸　✸　✸

There's a knock on my door. I open my eyes and yawn, realizing I fell asleep. I look at the clock. The door opens. I close my eyes.

"Willa," I hear Mother whisper, "are you awake?"

I don't answer.

My mother crosses the room. She tucks the thin summer comforter up under my chin. She kisses me gently on the forehead.

"Good night, Willa," she says.

I almost open my eyes. I almost tell her.

She turns off my night-light. I hear the door close.

Good night, Mom.

The worries flow back, the worries and the tears.

CHAPTER 13

The Orphans

✸ ✸ ✸

Alone, alone, all, all alone,
Alone on a wide wide sea!
— Samuel Taylor Coleridge

Pop, pop, pop, pop, pop! The sound of firecrackers somewhere outside wakes me up the next morning.

I open my eyes. It's the Fourth of July. Happy Independence Day.

I check my phone, still no messages. What?? I turn on my computer. There, yes.

Three messages from JFK. He lost his cell phone, "sorry." That explains it. He's started his internship, mostly grunt work, fetching gear and fly balls, but it's "all good." His grandparents have neighbors with grandkids his age, and he's already making some friends. Guy friends, I hope, but he doesn't say.

Someone's knocking on my door. "Come on in," I call.

It's Mother. "How are you feeling?" she asks.

"Better," I say, not making eye contact. "Thanks."

"Want to go for a run with me?" she says.

"Sure, Mom. Give me a minute and I'll meet you downstairs." I slip on shorts and a T-shirt, lace my sneakers, pull my hair back in a ponytail. I look at myself in the mirror. *Tell her, Willa.*

Outside we stretch and walk to warm up.

"Where's Salty?" Mom says. She knows he'd be the first in line for a morning run with us.

"I think he's with Sam," I say, feeling bad about lying, feeling worse about losing my dog.

Ruby's mother, Mrs. Sivler, is standing on the front step of No Mutts About It. She's wearing red strappy sandals, blue shorts, and a tight white camisole top, the picture of patriotism. Hands on her hips, she is muttering something to herself, shaking her head disgustedly.

"What's wrong, Mrs. Sivler?" I call over, then instantly wish I hadn't. What if Ruby told her mother about Will? What if Mrs. Sivler tells my . . .

"More orphans," Mrs. Sivler says, throwing up her hands, exasperated.

"What do you mean, Sherry?" my mother says, confused.

That makes two of us.

"Somebody left another basket of mangy mutts on our doorstep this morning. One of my workers called me to report it. Look at them." She points to the basket. "Skinny, scurvy little rats. What am I supposed to do with them?"

Rats? I walk over and look in the basket.

Kittens. Three adorable, just-born-looking orange kittens all curled up in a clump. "Oh, how cute," I say.

"Cute!" Mrs. Sivler says. "Eeew! No papers, pedigree, nothing. Why would somebody leave them here?"

"Well, this is a pet spa, Sherry," my mother says matter-of-factly with a pleasant smile.

I don't feel so neighborly. "Did you ever consider that maybe the owner couldn't afford to take care of them?" I snap.

Mother touches my arm, discreetly warning me not to be disrespectful.

"People are losing their jobs," I say. "Some families can't afford to feed their children, let alone their pets. Maybe—"

"Well, what am I supposed to do?" Mrs. Sivler sputters. Her perfect little white poodle, Pookie, runs out from the spa. She scoops him up in her arms, pulling him in tight to her ample chest so he won't have to bear the sight of those awful orphans in the basket. "Good morning, baby," she says. "How's Mommy's pookie-wookie snukum-pumpkin today? Did you have a nice bubble bath?"

"You could feed them," I say.

"Feed who?" Mrs. Sivler says.

"The kittens," I say. "I bet they'd like some milk or . . ."

My mother clears her throat. I look at her. I swear she almost laughed.

"Try calling the town, Sherry," Mother suggests. "The Bramble Animal Shelter. They'll come and get the kittens," she says. "Willa got her dog from that place. Very nice man runs it."

Salty Dog. I thought you were mine.

Mrs. Sivler snivels her upper lip up to meet her nostrils. "I suppose I could do that," she says. "Although it's certainly not my responsibility." She reaches into her pocket. She offers Pookie a treat.

One of the orphans makes a soft purring sound.

I look down at the kittens and smile. *You'll be okay, don't worry. They'll take good care of you at the shelter.*

Mother and I wait until we're a block away and then we burst out laughing.

"Can you believe that woman?" Mother says.

"The orphans," I say. "Wait till I tell Mariel." My throat clenches. *Where are you, Mariel?*

"I almost told her to send the kittens over to us," Mother says. "We've got a gang of barn cats they could join, but I wanted to see Sherry squirm a bit."

I laugh. My mother is surprising me. She actually has a sense of humor. Maybe this would be a good time to tell her about . . .

"Ready?" Mom says, adjusting her Red Sox cap, all set to run.

"Ready," I say.

"Let's go!" she says, and we're off.

Mother sets the pace. I try to keep up. My mom is a serious runner. I've only just recently started. My mother does 5 and 10K races for charity on the Cape and in the Boston area. She's even done some half marathons. She wants me to train and run the Falmouth Road Race with her next month. I doubt that I'll be ready, but I'm glad to have this time with my mother. She's usually so busy between running the inn and planning weddings that we don't spend much time together.

We head out along the water toward Popponesset Island.

"Willa, look," Mother calls back, pointing to a tall pole in the cove with a wooden perch on top.

The ospreys. "Yep, I see them," I shout. The two large brown and white hawks, the male and the female, are back again for the summer. Soon there will be a baby in that nest, nurtured and fed for the rest of the season until it's time to fly.

Back at the inn, Sam says Tina called me.

I assume she's going to start right in about meeting Will Havisham and "oh, my gosh, I didn't know you had a brother," but no, Tina blabs on and on about the lifeguards she and Ruby photographed up in Eastham and about the bonfire party on the beach tonight at six.

"You've got to come, Willa," Tina says. "Everybody will be there. Joey's in Florida, right? No reason you can't flirt with some college guys. A little flirting never hurt a sand fly, right? And wear something fun, will you? You're fourteen, not forty."

When I hang up with Tina, the phone rings again. Mariel!

"Oh, thank God, Mare. Where are you?"

"New York City," she says.

"What??!" I'm so surprised. "How did—"

"My mother sent for me, Willa," Mare says, sounding happier than I've ever heard her.

"Papa and the little ones are staying with cousins in Springfield. Mama sent money for the bus so I could come see her in Manhattan. Oh, Willa, it's just amazing here. I wish you could come. Maybe your parents would let you visit."

"I don't understand," I say. "Your mother's living in Manhattan?"

"Yes," Mariel says. "Mama finally hit the big time. She's starring in *Aqualina*. You've heard about it, right? The show with the mermaids and the—"

"Of course," I say. "It's the hottest musical on Broadway."

"I know," Mariel gushes. "And my mother's got the lead! The show is sold out until Christmas. Can you believe it, Willa? Isn't it wonderful? Mama says I can stay the whole summer."

I'm happy that my friend is happy, but my heart sinks into the sand nonetheless. First JFK is gone for the summer, now Mariel, too?

"Willa?" Mare says. "Are you okay? What's the matter?"

"Nothing," I say, not wanting to spoil a second of Mare's happiness. She's missed her mother for so long. I'm not going to rain on her Big Apple parade. "I'm just so happy for you, Mare, that's all."

"Thanks, Willa. I knew you'd be. You're such a good friend. I'll miss you! Have a nice holiday."

✳   ✳   ✳

On duty in the kitchen, I help Sam slide squares of marinated chicken and fresh-sliced chunks of potatoes, onion, and peppers from the garden onto long steel kabob skewers for tonight's holiday barbecue.

I work in silence, not looking at Sam, too afraid that if I start talking I'll gush out everything and fill up the kitchen with pity-party tears and worries, and Sam is far too busy with all of the holiday cooking preparations for that. There is potato salad and macaroni salad and baked beans to make. Corn to shuck. Watermelon to slice.

Mother prefers when Sam cooks gourmet nouvelle cuisine, but on days like the Fourth of July, people like the good old American traditional favorites. Hot dogs and hamburgers. Barbecue.

✳   ✳   ✳

After dinner, I head up to my room to dress for the bonfire. I sort through the clothes in my closet. Boring jean skirts and plain T-shirts, nothing flashy or sexy from a Hotties catalog.

I think about who will be at the bonfire. Who will I talk to? No JFK. No Mariel. Tina and Ruby strutting about side by side all night, flinging their mermaid hair, flirting with all the lifeguards, inseparable, best friends forever.

Suddenly I feel very, very alone.

CHAPTER 14

Bonfire on the Beach

They dined on mince, and slices of quince,
Which they ate with a runcible spoon;
And hand in hand, on the edge of the sand,
They danced by the light of the moon.
—Edward Lear

As I come up over the bluff to the beach just before sunset, I see the warm orange glow of the bonfire and hear music playing. At the top of the old, weather-worn gray beach stairs, I pause and look down.

The Buoy Boys are playing.

I don't see Tina or Ruby, but there are lots of other friends from school. Chandler and Caroline . . . Emily, Kelsie, Trish, Shefali, MacKenzie, and Allison.

Chandler and Caroline wave up at me. "Hey, Willa!"

That's nice. I walk down to join them.

We talk about how we did on our final exams. We laugh about the mermaid spotting. "Silly tourists," Caroline says.

Trish and Kelsie roast marshmallows. Shefali announces that her sister is engaged and maybe she'll get married at the Bramblebriar. Chandler asks who's entering the sand castle competition this year. "They always award trophies for the top three," she says.

I haven't built a sand castle in years. I think about Mariel's sweet sand castle story, about the mermaid wedding cakes. I hope Mare's having a good time in New York City with her mother. I am so happy for her.

A good song comes on. We start dancing. After a while, I start to unwind. I love to dance. Who needs a boyfriend? Who needs a best friend? When there's good music . . .

An unmistakable laugh. *Tina*.

I turn and look. Sure enough.

There is Tina Belle in full flirt mode. That would be Tina showing all of her beautiful, five-years'-worth-of-orthodontia, perfectly straight, brilliant white teeth all the way back to the molars.

Right now, Tina is flashing those molars at my brother. *Great*. Where's a lifeguard when you need one?

Will is sitting on a jetty rock, looking all British-movie-heartthrob handsome.

Tina pulls on his hand. "Come on, Will," she says, "let's dance."

I hear another unmistakable laugh, more like a barnyard cackle, actually.

Ruby. Of course.

Ruby Sivler is in full flirt mode, too. For Ruby, full flirt mode is wearing a limbo-low-cut top and shorts so short-short, if they were any shorter, they'd be invisible.

"Come on," Ruby says to Will, grabbing his free hand. "Dance with me."

Chandler makes a sucking-in-of-air sound.

"Uh-oh," says Caroline.

Suddenly the beach is silent. Tina and Ruby vying for the same boy?

Even the waves stop waving and listen.

Tina flips her blond hair back, period, end of sentence. She yanks on Will's hand. "Come on, Will. Let's go."

Ruby flips her red hair back, exclamation point. She pulls on Will's other hand. "Dance," she demands.

I look at my brother caught in the flirt-fire.

I actually feel a bit sorry for him.

Tina pulls on his left hand. Ruby pulls on his right.

Tina yanks harder. Ruby yanks more.

If Will were a wishbone, he'd snap.

I move forward to defend my brother from these bad, bad Cape Cod girls.

"That's enough," I say to Tina and Ruby. "Give it a break."

They look at me, shocked, not quite believing their ears.

"You heard me," I say. "Back off. He doesn't want to dance."

Everybody's watching. Tina and Ruby look around, embarrassed.

"Grow up, Willa, will you," Ruby says.

"Yeah, Willa," Tina says, trying to save face, too. "Grow up."

The two of them strut off in a huff. I notice they walk off in different directions. Good. Trouble in best-friends-forever land.

"What did you do that for?" Will says to me.

"Huh?" I'm confused. "I was helping you."

"Helping me? How? Keeping me from a night of snoggin' with two beautiful—"

"Snoggin'?" I say. "What's that?"

"Snoggin'," Will says as if I am stupid. "Snoggin'. Kissing. How old are you, anyway? Thanks a lot, Willa."

He shakes his head, annoyed, and walks off, most likely to find Tina and Ruby.

I turn to leave the party, feeling even more alone.

Snoggin'? Who knew?

Grow up, Willa. You're not four, you're fourteen. Everybody on the planet probably knows what snoggin' means.

When I reach the top of the beach stairs, four boys are getting out of an old Volvo station wagon. As they walk toward me, I see that they are college-age, lifeguards most likely. One's wearing a Boston College sweatshirt. "BC" is the college JFK wants to go to one day. JFK and a hundred thousand other kids.

As the lifeguards pass by I smell their cologne. They are joking with one another about something. I turn toward my bike, not wanting them to see me. I feel like I'm in kindergarten.

If Tina and Ruby were here, they'd already know these boys' names. They'd already be in on the joke. They'd know what they all did today and where they're staying. They'd know what cologne they are wearing.

Such a baby, Willa. Not even knowing what snoggin' meant.

I reach into the basket of my bike for the green stainless steel water bottle JFK gave me. I use this all the time now instead of all the plastic bottles that just get thrown away. I take a long drink.

"You're Willa, right?"

One of the college boys has stopped to talk to me.

He is movie-star, music-mogul, magazine-cover handsome. Dark-skinned, tall, built like a rugby player, faded jeans, white polo shirt, diamond stud earrings. He smiles. I nearly faint. My legs are like saltwater taffy.

"Go ahead down," the movie-star-music-mogul-magazine-model calls to his friends. "I'll catch up."

I gulp and take another drink of water.

The college boy leans in closer for a good look at my face. There aren't any lights in the parking lot, just the last wisps of the sunset and the glow of the fire from down below.

His eyes are brown and beautiful. I can't help but stare into them. There's light and motion in those eyes, like they're talking in some sort of sign language, *eye language*, conveying a wisdom and compassion that's somehow so familiar to me. . . .

"It is Willa, isn't it?" he says, smiling again.

Oh, my gosh, is he gorgeous. I find my voice. "Yes. How do you know me . . . my name?"

He laughs. "Oh, sorry, my bad." He extends his hand to shake mine. "I'm Robert—my friends call me Rob. You know my aunt. Sulamina Mum."

"Oh, my gosh," I say. "Mum? You're kidding! I thought I knew you somehow. I love Mum. I miss her. How is she? How's Riley? How's their new house—"

"Great," he says, shaking his head, laughing like he finds me amusing.

"Sorry," I say. "I talk fast when I get excited."

"No problem," he says. "That's sweet. You're sincere. Straight from the heart. That's what Aunt Sully said about you."

I have to look away from those mesmerizing brown eyes. I finger the locket around my neck to remind myself I have a boyfriend.

Rob runs his hand over his closely cropped black hair. "Aunt Sully told me to look you up when I got here. She sent me some pictures of you from her wedding."

"I was her maid of honor," I say.

Rob nods. "Yes. I wish I could have been there. Aunt Sully told me all about the Bramblebriar Inn, too. Sounds like a nice place."

"Where are you staying?" I ask.

"With my roommate, Brad. His family has a place in Mashpee. Brad talked me into lifeguarding here for the summer. We just got here today."

"Well, welcome to Cape Cod," I say. "I hope you have a great time."

"That's the plan," Rob says.

I hear girl voices.

Tina and Ruby are coming out of the restroom. They see me and Rob and their mouths drop. They look at Rob. They look at me. They look at Rob. They look at me, their eyes wide as teacup saucers.

Willa and the movie-star-music-mogul-magazine-model.

Tina and Ruby are so stunned that for once in their lives they are speechless.

Oh, how I wish I could savor this moment. But it's getting dark, and I need to bike home while there's still some light.

"I could show you around Bramble if you'd like," I say, savoring, savoring.

"That would be great, Willa, thanks."

I don't introduce Tina and Ruby. I pretend like they're not even there.

"What time are you done lifeguarding?" I ask, raising my voice to be sure Tina and Ruby can hear me.

"Five," he says.

"Come over for dinner, then," I say. "My mom and dad would love to meet you."

"I'd like that, thanks."

Rob takes off down the beach stairs to join his friends. I take a sip from my water bottle, drop it in my basket, hop on my seat, and sail.

Oh, my gosh, was that ever fun.

CHAPTER 15

The Widow's Walk

Her eyes the glow-worm lend thee,
The shooting stars attend thee;
And the elves also,
Whose little eyes glow
Like the sparks of fire, befriend thee.
— Robert Herrick

Biking home I'm giddy thinking about making Tina and Ruby jealous, but the feeling soon wears off as my mind starts remembering my worries.

Just a few weeks ago, at the start of the summer, everything felt so right. That was before JFK left for Florida. Before Mariel left for New York. Before Tina became Ruby's best friend. Before Will Havisham showed up and tipped my world upside down. Before Salty Dog turned traitor. Before the possibility that my birthfather might still be alive.

What happened to summer being simple and fun? Hot dogs and suntans and fireflies? Not this summer, oh, no. This summer makes me wish it were January.

It's dark when I get home. The inn is lit up so cheerily, though, huge American flag blowing in the breeze, smaller flags lining the driveway, white votive candles in sand-filled brown bags, pots of red geraniums in between.

Inside it's quiet, everyone off to a beach, no doubt, to watch a fireworks display. Just about every town on the Cape puts on a good show.

I know a spot where I can see several all at once. The widow's walk on the roof.

I head upstairs to the top floor of the inn, down the hall to Sam's office, still painted the cheery sunflower yellow color it was when he first showed me and Mother the estate, on that happy Fourth of July two years ago when Sam invited us here for a barbecue. It's a small room, small but big with books—wall-to-wall, floor-to-ceiling, shelves and shelves and shelves of Sam's favorite, page-frayed, finger-worn, much-loved books.

Sam's old mahogany sea captain's desk is cluttered with notebooks and stacks of papers. I'm sure there's a journal here somewhere. I'm tempted to look, but I don't. I would never want someone to read my private thoughts. I would never invade another's privacy.

I am curious, though, about "the book."

That first night we came here, Sam told me and Mother he was "working on a book." I was excited to ask him what he was writing, but Mother was babbling on about advice for renovating the building and we never got around to it. Sam kept turning the conversation back to Mother, back to me. That's Sam for you. Always putting other people first, drawing them out, focusing on them.

Over the past few years, I've noticed Sam scribbling notes here and there and I've asked him how his book is coming along, but he always changes the subject. Which of course makes me even more intrigued. Is it a book about the Cape? Fiction or nonfiction? Science fiction? Poetry? Mystery? Fantasy? A memoir?

I smile at the quote from Shakespeare's *The Tempest* on the wall:

My library was dukedom large enough.

The passageway up to the widow's walk is narrow, the stairs are steep. For a second I wonder about Sam's ancestors, Gracemore women of a century or more ago, who maybe climbed these same stairs, long skirts gathered up to keep from tripping, stepping out onto the widow's walk, hoping to catch a glimpse of a husband's boat safely home once more, praying the wild, ferocious sea had not that night made her a widow.

I smile, remembering how trembling excited I was that first Fourth of July night I walked up these stairs. Sam and Mother were getting along beautifully. I felt certain that finally, finally, this was the one. This was the man who would make my mother happy, the man who would be a wonderful husband for her, a wonderful father for me.

What if Billy Havisham is truly still alive?

How will Mother react?

How will Sam react?

When I push open the small door, the cool night air greets me and the wind gently strokes my cheeks. Above me is the black licorice sky, the vanilla cookie moon, a million sugar-speckled stars. Below is the endless, charcoal-dark ocean, some marshmallow whitecaps lit by lanterns from the bobbing boats poised in the harbor to watch the fireworks.

Over there is the town of Cotuit, that way, Falmouth; out there is the Woods Hole lighthouse, sending out its trusty beacon in a sure and steady beat; and there, way in the distance, are the lights of Martha's Vineyard.

I wonder, *Has Will gone home to the Southends' house or is he still at the bonfire with my friends? Why did you leave the party, Willa? That was your group, your friends.* I wonder if Mum's nephew, Rob, and his buddies joined in the bonfire party. Most likely. I'm sure Tina and Ruby have met Rob by now, their cute-guy radar going off the charts.

And here I am, alone.

I sigh and wrap my arms around me in a hug.

Look around you, Willa. Look, look. You are enmeshed in beauty—above you, below you . . . all around.

I breathe and smile and feel at peace.

How do I forget to stop and soak it in?

To be as small as a grain of sand in the midst of infinite grandeur.

For a moment I imagine Gramp Tweed "book-talking" with God and the angels in heaven. How silly we humans must seem, scurrying about with harried expressions, bundles of worries on our backs. When all around us there is—

Bang, bang, bang, shhhhhhhhhhh . . . The sky explodes now with sound and color and energy. One cannot describe fireworks with words. It happens too quickly, there is too much to hear, too much to see, too much to feel all at once. I think of JFK, somewhere in Florida, watching fireworks tonight. Of Mariel in Manhattan, maybe watching a show on the Hudson

River. Of my mother and Sam, no doubt linked arm in arm on their blanket on Falmouth Heights Beach. Of Nana visiting friends in Chatham tonight. Their eyes all glued to the sky. So many people who care about me. I am a lucky duck indeed.

My eyes fill with tears. *Thank you, God. Thank you. Thank you for reminding me how small I am. How safe I am. How very much I am loved.*

I wish I had my journal with me. I would try to write a few sentences to paint this picture around me. But some things can't be captured on a page. There aren't enough words, or maybe there are too many words. Maybe all a writer can really do is invite the reader to see. To please stand still and look. To stop, look, and listen. That funny little line I learned in nursery school, teaching us what to do before we crossed the street.

There's a volley of firecrackers in a backyard a few houses down. I see a young girl holding a sparkler, her expression so carefree, happy.

Enjoy it, little girl, enjoy it. Every little spark, every second.

You'll grow up soon enough, and nothing will feel simple again.

✶ ✶ ✶

I crawl into bed and choose a new skinny-punch.

A classic. *The Pearl* by John Steinbeck. A poor fisherman finds a pearl and suddenly his life is changed forever.

"In the town they tell the story of the great pearl—how it was found and how it was lost again. . . . And, as with all retold tales that are in people's hearts, there are only good and bad things and black and white things and good and evil things and no in-between anywhere."

I read for hours, listening to the sounds of guests coming in for the night downstairs, voices talking, laughing, faucets running, toilets flushing.

There's a knock on my door.

Mom and Sam. Stopping to say good night. Sam has his arm around my mother in the doorway, their happy faces lit by the hallway sconce.

"Love you, Willa," Mom says.

"Love you," Sam says.

"Love you, too," I say. "Good night."

What if my birthfather, Mother's first husband, is really still alive? What if that destroys their happiness? Breaks up our perfect family? I think about how they had a miscarriage earlier this summer. I remember how happy I was to think that maybe, after being an only child my whole life, I might finally have a little sister or brother.

I write in my journal and mull and worry. *Willa the Warrior*, I remind myself. Tomorrow I will talk to Mother. I owe her that. Surely by now Tina and Ruby have told their parents. This town is so small. Mother deserves to hear such shocking news from me, her daughter, not that blabbermouth pooch-queen Sherry Sivler.

There, I feel better now. I have a plan. Action, not worry, that's the key.

I reopen Steinbeck's *The Pearl* and dive back in, reading, reading, reading until the Bramblebriar Inn is hushed for the night. Only the crickets still cricketing outside.

When I reach the last line, I sigh and smile.

"And the music of the pearl drifted to a whisper and disappeared."

I close the cover and savor the moment.

Savoring, savoring . . . oh, to write a book like that.

CHAPTER 16

The Labyrinth

✳ ✳ ✳

Here's flowers for you;
Hot lavender, mints, savoury, marjoram;
The marigold, that goes to bed wi' the sun
And with him rises weeping: these are the flowers
Of middle summer. . . .
　　　　　　　—Shakespeare

When I seek out my mother the next morning, Darryl, who's managing the front desk today, says she's over at Bramble United Community with a couple from upstate New York who are having their reception here on Saturday.

"After that, she's off-Cape for the afternoon," Darryl says. "Meeting with a bride-to-be in Boston, I think. She did say she'd be back in time for dinner."

Dinner, that reminds me. I need to find Sam and make sure it's okay that I invited Mum's nephew, Rob, for dinner.

Sam is filling bird feeders out by the Labyrinth. The Labyrinth is a walking circle Sam designed when he first took over the estate. You enter between two spruce shrubs and follow a narrow path bordered by perennial flowers and bushes, walking in toward the center, then back out toward the border, circling in and away, in and away, until you reach the stone bench in the middle. If you stay on the path, you can't get lost. A good metaphor for life, I think.

Sam's flowers are full-bloom beautiful in every color of the rainbow: red, yellow, pink, blue, purple, orange, and white. The smell of lavender is everywhere. A fat blue jay lands in one of the birdbaths, splashing water everywhere.

I tell Sam about Rob.

"Oh, that's wonderful," Sam says. "Of course he's welcome. Good timing, too. Rosie's handling the kitchen tonight. It's my night off. Your mother and I were looking forward to having dinner with you. We've all been so busy this summer, we haven't had much time to really talk."

"Talk about what?" I ask.

"Nothing special," Sam says.

When he turns back to pour seeds in another feeder, I see him smile.

"What, Dad? Tell me."

Sam laughs. "Later, Willa. Nothing that can't wait."

✳   ✳   ✳

After my shift in the kitchen, I head up to my room to check my messages.

None from JFK, but there's this chatty little voice mail from a girl named "Lorna" who wants to know, "What's Joey's favorite kind of birthday cake?"

What?

She's throwing him a surprise party for his birthday Friday night at the country club their grandparents all belong to. "We all love him. He's such a sweetie."

What! My jealousy hits the high jump. *I love him.* He's *my* sweetie.

Lorna says Joey mentioned me "once or twice" and she got my number from his cell phone.

He only mentioned me *once or twice*? What's she doing with his cell phone? I start to text her back, angry and annoyed, then Reason throws a roadblock.

Reason: Maybe she's just trying to be nice, Willa.

Willa: Let her be nice to someone else's boyfriend.

Reason: Maybe she's ugly with green teeth and horrendous breath and . . .

Willa: She's probably gorgeous.

Reason: It is JFK's birthday and he is far away from home and probably bored to death hanging out with his grandparents.

Willa: Nothing wrong with boring. Boring's good. We'll have fun when he gets back to Bramble. I'll throw him a surprise party—

Reason: *Willa.*

Willa: What?

Reason: You're being selfish. It's his birthday.

Willa: Oh, all right, all right. You win. Again.

I text back Lorna Doone. "Hi, Lorna, that's nice of you to throw a party for Joseph. He likes chocolate cake with chocolate frosting. His favorite ice cream is mint chocolate chip." I resist saying "Tell him his girlfriend says hello."

After lunch I head into town to buy a birthday card for JFK. I stop by the new dollar store and purchase four clear plastic containers with yellow tops. They look like oversize mayonnaise jars to me, gallon-size, but the sticker says they are for "sun tea." They'll do just fine.

At home, I get the sharpest knife I can find in the kitchen and I cut holes, jaggedly but they'll do, into the center of each lid. I get a fat black marker and write CHANGE FOR GOOD ✪ on each jug.

I put mine on my dresser, next to the photo of Billy Havisham.

All those years I looked at this picture wondering about the man who was my father. Often having nightmares about how awful it must have been to have crashed and drowned all alone in the ocean like that.

"If you're alive, where have you been? Why didn't you ever come to meet me? Why haven't you told Mother? What kind of man are you, anyway?"

I put the photo in my dresser drawer and slam it shut. I don't want to see those eyes. *Sparkling like the sea on a sunny summer day.*

I smile at the CHANGE FOR GOOD ✪ jug. I like that name. Maybe I can start a trend here. I empty out my jacket pockets, fish around my dresser, desk, backpack, purses. The pennies, nickels, dimes, and quarters make a satisfying clinking sound as I drop them in. It will take a long time to fill, but I've made a start on my next way to serve. I can't wait to tell Mum.

Sam smiles when I offer him his CHANGE FOR GOOD ✪ jug.

"Great idea, Willa," he says. "Simple and easy to use. I like it. Thanks. What will we use the money for?"

"I think each person should decide that for him- or herself," I say. "There are so many organizations, important causes. I think we should each use what we collect toward something we believe in."

Sam smiles. "I'm proud of you, Willa. Always finding a way to pay your community rent."

Community rent is a phrase Sam uses to suggest that each person in society has an obligation to give back in some way. Whether it's to your local or national or global community . . . it doesn't matter, just as long as you pay your rent—your fair share of time, talent, or resources.

"I'll put this on my dresser and start filling it tonight," Sam says.

"Can you take Mom's jug, too?" I say.

"Maybe you'd like to give it to her yourself," Sam says. He winks at me. "Explain your good idea."

"Oh, sure," I say, smiling. Sam is always finding little ways to get my mother and me to spend more time together, to talk more. My mother and I don't have the best history of getting along, but lately we're starting to connect more.

After lunch I fill out JFK's birthday card and put it in the mailbox. Upstairs on my bed I choose a new skinny-punch. *Tuck Everlasting* by Natalie Babbitt. The opening line is gorgeous:

The first week of August hangs at the very top of summer, the top of the live-long year, like the highest seat of a Ferris wheel when it pauses in its turning.

I stop and picture me and JFK at the Barnstable Fair, holding hands in our seat on the Ferris wheel, paused up at twelve midnight, me begging him not to rock the carriage, him teasing me like he will, our feet dangling free in the summer night air. I look down at all the lights below us and then he kisses me.

I pull out my bag of candy from my nightstand, open a taffy, peppermint, pop it in, and continue reading. The story is about a girl named Winnie who meets a family who has found the secret to eternal life. I underline sections I want to remember and I mark up the margins with "wow" and "beautiful" and "love that." On page eighty-six, the character Miles says: *"Someday . . . I'll find a way to do something important."*

Next to his words I write "me, too, I hope!"

It's a lovely summer evening. Rosie has set an extraspecial pretty table for me and Mother and Sam and Rob out by the Labyrinth. To please my mother,

I've dressed up a bit, a yellow skirt and a white cotton eyelet blouse.

Rosie has prepared an entrée of pasta with grilled chicken, broccoli, tomatoes, and feta cheese, seasoned with Kalamata olives. A fresh green salad dotted with cranberries. Warm baguettes with butter. Peach cobbler for desert.

Rob is right on time, dressed in a white collared polo shirt and long, tan pants. So handsome. He hands Sam a bottle of wine and gives my mother a box of candy with the familiar gold SWEET BRAMBLE BOOKS label.

"Oh, how thoughtful of you, Rob," Mother says. "Thank you."

Rob smiles. "I didn't know your mother owned the candy store. You probably have more candy than you need."

"Never enough candy," I say, and we all laugh.

"Let's sit," Sam says. He passes the salad bowl to Rob.

"We were so delighted you could join us for dinner," Mom says.

"Thank you," Rob says. He takes a bite of salad. "Delicious."

"You're on break from Boston College, Willa tells us," Sam says. "What are you majoring in?"

"I haven't declared yet," Rob says, "but I'm leaning toward history and political science. I was president of my class this year. I'm not sure yet, but I may want to run for public office someday."

"That's wonderful," Sam says.

"How are you finding our small town?" Mother asks.

"Great," Rob says. "Everyone is so friendly. I was glad to run into Willa last night at the beach." He turns to me.

"Willa, your friends Tina and Ruby are a riot. And your brother—"

Time stops.

My mother coughs. She takes a drink of water. "What did you say? Willa's *brother*?"

"Yes," Rob says. "His name is Will, right? I was surprised Aunt Sully hadn't mentioned him. Good guy. I thought maybe he'd be here tonight."

I'm underwater, underwater, ears plugging, I can't breathe.

"What are you talking about?" Mother demands. "Willa doesn't have a brother. She's an only child."

"Stella," Sam says. He puts his hand on Mother's arm. "It's okay. Surely there's some mistake."

"I know," I blurt out. "You must be talking

about my friend Jessie. He's always joking around like that, saying he's my brother because we look so much alike." I turn my face away from Mom and Sam, using eye language with Rob to say, "Please just go along with me."

Rob gets my message. "Oh, sorry," he says. "My mistake. I knew Aunt Sully would have mentioned a brother. She's always talking about your family and how much she misses all of you."

"How is Mum?" Sam asks, nicely diverting the conversation. *Thank you, Sam.* "Tell us all the news."

There's an icy aura about my mother. She takes a disinterested bite of her dinner. She looks worlds away in thought. I can almost see the questions circling around like a labyrinth in her brain.

After dessert, I walk Rob out to the front gate to try to explain to him what's going on. He says to let him know if there's any way he can be of help.

"I'll be working on South Cape Beach all the rest of the week," he says. "Come by anytime if you need me."

In bed, I toss and turn, falling in and out of sleep. I'm riding on a Ferris wheel, all alone, circling round and round. . . . The wheel breaks away from the axis and now I'm spinning out over the ocean, higher, higher up and then *whoosh*, I'm headed down. Down,

down, down. Oh, my gosh, I'm going to drown! *Wake up, Willa, wake up.* I bolt upright in bed, sweating, shaking. What do I do now?

I get out of bed. I find the slip of paper with Will Havisham's number on it and call him. When he answers, I tell him to meet me on the beach tomorrow morning at eight and to bring money and his leads about our birthfather and his driver's license so we can rent a car.

CHAPTER 17

The Road Trip

✦ ✦ ✦

I have been here before,
But when or how I cannot tell:
I know the grass beyond the door,
The sweet keen smell,
The sighing sound, the lights around the shore.
— Dante Gabriel Rossetti

As soon as Will's boat is anchored in the morning, I hit him with it straight out. "If our father is alive, and he's here on Cape Cod, let's find him."

Will stares at me. "Are you sure you're up for this?"

"Where's Salty?" I ask, looking past him into the boat.

"On the Vineyard, at the Southends' house."

I can barely hide my tears.

"Oh, Willa," he says. "I'm so sorry. I know how much you must miss him. That day Salty jumped out of the boat and swam to shore straight to you . . . I was shocked. He never did anything like that before. It's like he knew you were my sister."

"He is a very smart dog," I say, sniffling.

"Sure is," Will says. "I trained him, didn't I? He's been my family, Willa. He's all I've got. Until I find my father, that is."

I look at Will. Our eyes meet, blue to blue. What if he's right? What if we find Billy Havisham today? I shiver, not knowing whether I'm excited or just plain scared.

First stop. Hyannis. There was a meeting of an international organization of people in the advertising field held here two years ago this month. The title of the conference was "What's the Big Idea?"

That was the name of our father's company.

We track down a woman at the Convention and Visitors Bureau. She remembers booking the group. "What a fun bunch of people," she says with a laugh. "Especially the ones from New York. They were wild." She checks the file. No. No one by the name of William Frederick "Billy" Havisham.

Out on the main street, Will sees the signs for the John F. Kennedy Museum. "Mind if we stop?" he says.

"Sure." I've been many times, but I always find it inspirational.

As we look at the photographs of the Kennedy

family, I think of my JFK, how his birthday is tomorrow, how I hope he gets my card in time, how I hope that cookie girl has gross teeth and facial warts.

Next stop. Chatham. Will has a clipping from a newspaper story dated four years ago. There was a famous author in town, Stephen King, and there was a long line of people waiting to meet him at a bookstore on Main Street.

"Right there, see," Will says, pointing to a man in the line in the newspaper photo. The man's face is turned downward. He is reading from a book as he waits to talk with the author.

It's hard to tell, but I agree that there is a resemblance to our father.

When we reach the bookstore, Yellow Umbrella, we ask to speak with the owner. We show him the clipping. He nods. Yes, of course he remembers Stephen King's visit, but no, he's sorry, he's never seen the man in the picture.

"I know pretty much everyone in Chatham," he says. "Most likely he was a tourist."

✸   ✸   ✸

We get back into the car and continue up Route 28. We see a sign for BOX LUNCHES and stop for sandwiches. We eat in the car on the way out toward the

Outer Cape. I tear open Will's bag of Cape Cod chips to make it easy for him as he's driving.

"These are good," he says.

"The best," I say.

We're headed out to the National Seashore, a more than twenty-mile-long gorgeous expanse of beaches federally protected from commercial development by President John F. Kennedy. I have Will pull in to my favorite beach, Nauset Beach, so he can see how beautiful it is.

The surfers are already at it, riding the best waves on the Cape. Folks are lined up at Liam's for fried clams and hot dogs and shakes.

Back in the car, I read through Will's clippings about the "dune shacks"—a group of cottages built on a two-mile strip of dunes in Truro and Provincetown at the far end of the Cape. Sam has mentioned them a few times and I've always been intrigued. The cottages were built by the coast guard in the early 1900s to serve as temporary shelters for people stranded in storms. Over the years, the dune shacks became retreats for such famous writers as Jack Kerouac, Norman Mailer, and Eugene O'Neill.

"This is so interesting," I say.

"You're in good company," Will says.

"What do you mean?" I say.

"You . . . wanting to be a writer someday."

"How did you know that?" I say.

Will laughs. "Your friend Tina told me. What a chatterbox that one is. Pretty though, really really. But I already knew about you wanting to be a writer."

"How?" I ask.

"All the clues," Will says. "Saving that old library you love. Writing letters to the newspapers. Putting those quotes out on that board in front of the inn. What do you call that thing?"

"The Bramble Board," I say. *Tina talked about me wanting to be a writer someday? That was nice of her.*

"You should put your own words up there," Will says. "On that Bramble Board."

"Maybe, someday," I say. "When I have something important to say."

"I bet you do already," Will says.

I smile and look out the window. *That was nice of him. I'm growing to like this long-lost brother of mine. Even if he did take my dog away.*

Reason: It was *his* dog.

Willa: I know, I know. Be quiet.

I keep reading the news clippings. In recent years, the "dune dwellers"—people who come back year after year to spend time at one of the nineteen cottages — have unsuccessfully sought legal protection for what they feel are their long-term rights, sort of like old-fashioned "squatter's rights" to the dwellings.

I hold one clipping toward the sunlight streaming through the rental car window to get a better look at a picture of a particular man.

Will looks over at me. "That's right. That's the one. It's him. Isn't it?"

I stare at the face. Too bad the picture is in black-and-white. If I could only see the eyes. Nonetheless, this guy does indeed look like an older version of the man in the photo on my dresser.

"Ice cream?" Will says, pointing to a sign up ahead.

"Sure." It's always a good time for ice cream.

We stop at Sundae School, one of my favorite places. Will gets rum raisin. I get my usual Heath bar crunch.

"Clever name for an ice cream store," Will says. "Sundae School."

I nod, thinking about our birthfather, about how he made his living coming up with clever names and advertising slogans.

"Hand me my backpack, will you," Will says.

He fishes around inside and pulls out a book. "Here," he says. "A present."

Skellig by David Almond.

"He's one of my favorite authors," Will says. "I thought you'd enjoy it."

I scan the back cover. "Sounds good, Will. Thanks."

"You're welcome," he says with a smile. "I know how much you love to read."

He's nice. Really nice.

"I'd love to visit England someday," I say. "See the Globe Theatre where Shakespeare's plays were performed, visit the birthplaces of Dickens and Jane Austen and—"

"Come visit me, then," he says, all excited. "Please. The castle is empty most of the year. My grandparents are always traveling. Just me and the twenty-two butlers and maids."

"Really?" I say. "Twenty-two?"

"Well, maybe there are only thirteen."

The farther out we drive, the fewer buildings we see, and then finally there are just long stretches of sand, like one big, long beach.

When we reach the dune shacks, Will parks the car and we get out. The wind has picked up, clouds moving in.

"I feel like I've been here before," Will says, looking around. "Have you ever had that happen? You are someplace you've never been before, yet it's like you have been?"

"Yes," I say. "Déjà vu. It happens to me often."

I feel a raindrop, and then another. "Let's go," I say.

We knock on a cottage door.

No one answers.

We try another, and another.

No luck.

I feel more drops. "We should go," I say.

"Wait," Will says. "Look."

There's a man coming out of one of the cottages. We go to him and tell him our story. He says that he and his wife have lived here for more than fifty years. He invites us inside, offers us lemonade.

Will shows him photos of our birthfather.

"No, no," the old man says, shaking his head. "Not familiar."

"Well, what about these," Will says, his voice still hopeful.

Will hands the old man the clipping about these dune shacks . . . the picture of the man who looks like our father. I look at Will's face. He's so hopeful.

The old man shakes his head. "No, sorry, kids. That's my friend Eric. He's been coming here for years."

I look at Will. He drops his gaze. I can feel his disappointment.

Rain is beating steadily on the cottage roof. "We better get back, Will."

Driving home, my brother doesn't say a word. I feel bad for him.

He looks sad, so broken down. Me? I actually feel relieved. If my birthfather is dead, then my life can go on just as happily as ever.

I have a father. I have a mother.

If Billy Havisham is dead, Will is an orphan.

"I'm not giving up so easily," Will says, as if he can read my thoughts.

"I know," I say, "but you should prepare yourself for —"

"No," he says. "I'm not preparing myself for anything except finding my father. Our father."

When we get back to Bramble, I tell Will to drop me off in town, at the library. I can't risk my mother seeing him leaving me at the inn. As soon as I get home, the very first chance I get, I'm going to tell her everything.

Dr. Swaminathan and Mrs. Saperstone are coming out of the library. Dr. Swammy flicks open an oversize plaid umbrella. He offers Mrs. Saperstone his elbow and she inches in next to him. What a cute couple they make.

Dr. Swammy escorts her down the steps. They are smiling. He says something and she laughs. I've seen them sitting together at BUC on Sundays, Dr. Swammy buying her candy, going to programs she runs at the library.

They look so happy together. They look like they're in love.

Boing, I can hear cupid's arrow. I knew it! Good. Two of my favorite people. Maybe I'll have another wedding to plan before the summer is out.

They see me and insist I join them under the umbrella.

"No, thanks," I say, "I'm going to make a run for it."

I'm soaking wet when I get home.

Mother is waiting for me at the door.

The minute I see the expression on her face, I know she knows about Will.

She stares at me, eyes filled with pain, shaking her head like she is so disappointed in me, like how could I have hurt her so badly.

"Mom . . . I . . ."

"Get some dry clothes on and meet me in my room," she says.

CHAPTER 18

Horrible, No-Good, Awful Daughter

* * *

No tears in the writer, no tears in the reader.
—Robert Frost

"Why didn't you tell me about Will Havisham?" Mother asks, her eyes filling with tears.

My mother is not one to cry. I feel even worse, if that's possible. I slink down to sit on her bed, head in my hands, a horrible, no-good, awful daughter.

"I had to hear it in the grocery store, from Sherry Sivler of all people."

"I'm sorry, Mom. Really I am. I wanted to tell you but first I needed to make sure that it was true."

"And then Tina's mother calls me today. It seems the whole town knows before I—"

"Mom, I'm sorry. I didn't want you to be hurt."

"Does he really look just like you?" Mom says, her voice cracking.

I nod my head, yes.

My mother walks to the window. "And he's British?" Mom says.

I nod my head, yes.

"What's he doing here on Cape Cod?" my mother says, walking back to face me. "How did he know where we were living? How did he find you? I can't believe this. Why . . ." She stops, lets out a choked sob. She walks back to the window.

There's a knock on the door. Sam pokes his head in. "There's a young couple downstairs to see you, Stell," he says. "Denise and Scott. You have a meeting with them about their wedding Saturday?"

Mom checks her watch. "Oh, my gosh, I nearly forgot. Show them to the library, Sam. Tell them I'll be there in a few minutes. Maybe you could get them some iced tea or something."

"Sure thing, sweetheart," Sam says. "No problem." Sam looks at me and smiles the kindest, sweetest smile. He looks at Mom and winks.

Oh, no, Sam. Your life is about to change and you don't even know it. If Billy Havisham is still alive, then . . .

"We only have a few minutes, Willa. Tell me quickly."

"Sure, Mom. Sit down. I'll tell you everything I know."

✷ ✷ ✷

My mother cries when I tell her about Annie Bolton.

"He was spending so much time in Europe," Mother says. "Before and after we met. Opening up branches of his company . . ."

"She broke it off with him," I say. "Her family forced her to. They wanted her to marry this other really wealthy guy."

"What people will do for money," Mother says, standing up, moving to the window again.

When I tell her about Will's mother dying, Mom shakes her head. "Poor boy. Losing both of his parents."

"Well . . ." I say, and then stop.

"Well, what?" Mother asks.

"Nothing." My heart is pounding. "That's all."

"Tell me, Willa," Mother says, her mother radar revving into high gear.

Go ahead, Willa, out with it. Enough secrets. She has a right to know.

This time I don't argue with Reason. This time Reason is right.

"Mom," I say with a weak smile. "You'd better sit down."

Mother does as I ask.

Straight out, Willa. That's the best way.

"Mom . . . I think my birthfather . . . your first husband . . . Billy Havisham . . . there's a chance he might still be alive."

Mother lets out a long, loud sigh.

That's odd. I'm not sure, but it almost seems like she is relieved. *How could that be?*

"I've got to meet that couple downstairs," Mom says, standing up and heading toward the door. "I'll come to your room to talk when they're gone."

"Okay," I say, "I'll be waiting."

"It may take a while," Mother says.

I feel so bad for her, having to put on her polished, all-in-control wedding planner business face when her heart must just be shattering inside.

"You know these engaged couples," Mother says. "All those pre-wedding jitters and questions and worries as the *big day* finally approaches. I may be hand-holding till midnight."

"I know, Mom." I nod, wedding planner to wedding planner. "Take your time. I'll wait up."

When she goes I head to my room and rush for my journal, writing as the tears pour down. I would give anything to hug my dog right now.

I picture Salty staring at me as I wrote or read, one eye cocked higher than the other, eager for any sign that I would come to my senses and take him outside.

"I miss you, Salty." More and more tears come.

I think of JFK, of Mariel, of Mum so far away, but most of all right now, I just want my dog.

CHAPTER 19

And at night I love listening to the stars.
It's like five-hundred million little bells. . . .

— Antoine de Saint-Exupéry

There's a knock on the door.

Sam. "I brought you some dinner," he says.

A tuna sandwich with macaroni salad and Cape Cod chips, a tall glass of soda, and a slice of Rosie's scrumptious chocolate cake with chocolate frosting. For a second I think of JFK. Of the birthday cake that girl Lorna is surprising him with.

"Are you okay?" Sam asks.

"Mom told you?" I say.

"Yes," Sam says. He sets the tray on my nightstand, smiling as he moves the mountain stack of skinny-punch books to the floor.

"Glad you've got a book or two to read," he says.

I laugh. "You know me and my books, Dad."

My voice breaks at the word *Dad*. I think of how I

130

spent the day with my new brother, Will, on a wild goose chase for our birthdad.

"It must have been quite a shock to hear you have a half brother," Sam says.

I study his face. I can tell Sam doesn't know I might have a father alive, too. He doesn't know about Billy Havisham.

I hope Mother's meeting doesn't take too long. I can't bear the waiting.

"It's funny," Sam says.

"What?" I say.

"Funny's not the right word," Sam says. "Just a strange coincidence. The other night, when your mom and I wanted to have dinner alone with you—"

"You were going to tell me something," I say, remembering.

Sam nods his head with a sweet-sad smile.

"What, Dad? Tell me."

"We were going to tell you that we have decided to start the adoption process. After the miscarriage, we thought long and hard about things. At our age, having a baby can be risky. And there are so many children already in the world just waiting for a family, praying every day that a family will adopt them."

"Oh, Dad, that's wonderful! Is it a boy? A girl? A baby or an older—"

Sam laughs. "Whoa, whoa, whoa," he says. "We haven't gotten that far yet. Deciding to adopt was a huge decision. We're still adjusting to that. One step at a time."

When I finish eating dinner, I put my tray outside the door, feeling like a Bramblebriar guest rather than one of the owners.

Mother may be a while. I might as well have a little book fest while I'm waiting.

I check out my skinny-punch pile on the floor. The cover of *The Little Prince* by Antoine de Saint-Exupéry catches my eye.

It looks like a kid's book, but shortly after I begin reading, I realize it is one of those ageless, timeless classics . . . like Shel Silverstein's *The Giving Tree*, which holds meaning for every reader, no matter how old. I want to write a book like that someday. A skinny book with a punch.

There's a good thought on page sixty-three that I copy into my book of quotes:

*"One sees clearly only with the heart.
Anything essential is invisible to the eyes."*

I check the clock, still early. I take my crumpled bag of candy from my nightstand drawer—almost time for a refill. I pop a sticky red fish into my mouth, remembering Jimmy of the Gummy Worms, and choose another book: *The House on Mango Street* by Sandra Cisneros.

It is so beautifully written. It reads like poetry. I jot down lines I like in my journal.

Page 11: *"She looked out the window her whole life, the way so many women sit their sadness on an elbow."*

Page 33: *"You can never have too much sky."*

Page 61: *"You must keep writing. It will keep you free."*

Page 87: *"One day I'll own my own house, but I won't forget who I am or where I came from."*

Page 105: *"When you leave you must remember to come back for the others. A circle, understand?"*

I love this book. Definitely makes the Willa's Pix List.

I get up and dress for bed. Looking out my window, I gaze up at the stars. *I wish I may, I wish I might.* I try to hear them like the Little Prince does, but they are silent.

I unwrap the last three pieces of saltwater taffy and choose a new skinny-punch book. *42 Miles* by Tracie Vaughn Zimmer. There's a girl's face and a map on the cover. *Where is she going?* I wonder.

The first page tells me that the main character is facing big changes in her life. The second page starts:

I look just like Mom—
hazel eyes
straight brown hair.
Even my dimples
match hers.

My chest tightens. I close the book.

Why do I have to look just like my birthfather? Why can't I look just like my mother? Maybe then I wouldn't be such a painful reminder to her.

I finish the book quickly. On the page inside the front cover I write: "I like how JoEllen brings the half of herself she is in her mother's house and the half of herself she is in her father's house together to make a whole. Gorgeous writing, vibrant, fresh, and hopeful."

I get a drink of water. Brush my teeth. Still no Mom. I remember the book Will gave me today, still in my beach bag.

I open *Skellig* and read the first line. *"I found him in the garage on a Sunday afternoon."* The plot is engaging, the language lyrical, each chapter a quick, tight scene. I keep writing "nice" in the margins.

A knock on my door. My breath catches.

Finally. This is it. "Come on in, Mom."

CHAPTER 20

Gifts from My Father

✳ ✳ ✳

If I chance to talk a little wild, forgive me;
I had it from my father.
— Shakespeare

Straight out, I tell her. How Will thinks Billy Havisham is still alive. About Will's folder full of newspaper clippings and clues. About our road trip around the Cape today checking out possible leads.

"Oh, Willa," Mother says, coming to sit next to me on my bed. "I wish you had talked with me. I could have spared you. . . ." She looks away.

"Spared me what?"

"Billy Havisham is dead," she says.

"But it's possible. . . ."

"No." Mother shakes her head. "It's not. Your father died in a hot-air balloon crash the day after our wedding."

"But are you sure?" I say. "His body was never recovered. What if he survived somehow and—"

"No, Willa. He didn't."

"How do you know?" I say, my voice rising. "Maybe he struck his head and got amnesia and when rescuers found him he didn't know his name and—"

"No, honey. That didn't happen. He's dead. That's all."

"But what if you're wrong, Mom?" I shout, my voice cracking.

"Willa." My mother brushes my hair off my forehead. She stares at me. "Look at those eyes. Those beautiful blue eyes. Just like his."

"I know, I know," I say angrily. "The one and only good thing."

"Willa . . . no," Mother says. "You have your father's boundless enthusiasm. And his beautiful way with words. You get those gifts from your father."

My eyes fill with tears. "But maybe, just maybe, he is still alive." My whole body is shaking with conflicted feelings, like the point at Poppy Spit where the ocean current meets the mild bay, swirling, swirling.

"Wait here, Willa," Mother says. "I need to get something."

Moments later, she returns. She hands me a folder. I open it.

A letter from the US Coast Guard "regretting to inform . . ." I read through to the end. They searched and dredged the waters for miles around. They found articles of his clothing, his wallet, and then, horribly, something washed up onshore farther up the coast two days later. A severed limb, Billy's leg, with clear evidence of shark mutilation.

"Oh, my gosh." I gasp, feeling sick to my stomach.

"I know, honey," Mother says, touching my arm.

"But why didn't you ever tell me this?"

"I'm sorry, Willa," she says. "Maybe it was wrong not to tell you, but I didn't want you having nightmares. He was dead and that was all. I know you, sweetheart. I imagined you'd play the awful story out over and over again in your beautiful imagination. I didn't want that scary, tragic ending in your mind." Mother makes a squeaking sound. Her lips tremble.

"I know you found the love letters and poems, oh, those poems Billy wrote to me," Mother says.

"In the Valentine's box in your closet," I say.

Mother nods and smiles.

"How did you know I found them?"

Mother laughs. "Mother magic," she says. "I know you tried on my wedding gown, too. You used to leave candy wrappers, always a telltale sign that my sweet daughter was around."

"Cherry cordials," I say. "They used to be my favorite."

"Oh, I know!" Mother says. "You and those cherry pits."

We laugh, remembering how a certain incident involving cherry cordials and me and a famous soap opera star's wedding gown got my mother into a hornet's nest of trouble and nearly ruined her career as a wedding planner.

I look at my mother. She smiles at me. I think of how much we have been through together. I start to cry. My mother hugs me.

"I love you, Willa," she whispers in my ear.

"I love you, too, Mom."

My mother holds me close, rocking us back and forth, and in our silence we fill a book with so many unspoken words.

CHAPTER 21

Mum's Advice

The heart can push the sea and land
Farther away on either hand;
The soul can split the sky in two,
And let the face of God shine through.
— Edna St. Vincent Millay

When I wake Friday morning, I feel good about the talk with Mother last night, but nonetheless my heart is heavy.

There is something important I need to do today and I am dreading it.

To crush someone's dream . . . someone's greatest hope . . . seems the cruelest task I've ever had to face. I don't know that I can go through with it.

July 7. JFK's birthday. Too early to call. I leave him a happy birthday text message and promise I'll call him later. I hope his card gets there today. I hope that girl Lorna gets a bad case of halitosis and can't make

the surprise party tonight after all and it's just a couple of guy friends who show up.

Willa, Reason starts in.

"I know, I know, I know."

After I finish working the breakfast shift, I pack a lunch and bike out to South Cape Beach. That's where the sand castle competition will be tomorrow. I'm sure I won't run into Will here. I need some time to think first.

Sulamina Mum's nephew, Rob, is coming out of the lifeguard headquarters with a clipboard and a megaphone, beach towel around his neck.

"Willa," he says, "hey."

I walk with him down to his station. I tell him what Mother told me about my birthfather last night.

"Oh, I'm sorry," he says. He reaches out to touch my arm, his brown eyes full of sincere compassion. He reminds me so much of Mum, I start to cry. Just then, out of the corner of my eye, I see Tina and Ruby.

"Hey, hey," Rob says, hugging me, "don't cry."

I squint through my tears. Tina and Ruby have stopped dead in their tracks. *Oh, my gosh, how funny.* They think Rob likes me.

"I'm okay," I say to Rob, flinging back my hair, looking into his eyes with a great big smile. "You made me think of Mum, how much I miss her."

Rob uses a corner of his beach towel to dry a tear from my face.

I can almost feel the jealous stares. *This is fun.*

Rob notices Tina and Ruby. Tina has a notebook and pen in her hands. Ruby has her camera. Two budding bestselling authors aiming to write another chapter featuring a handsome Cape Cod lifeguard.

"Oh, no," Rob says, turning his back to them. "Here they come again."

"Again?"

"Yeah, they were here yesterday trying to get me to be in this book they're making. I said no."

"Why?" I say. "You sure belong in it."

"What if I want to run for president someday? That's all I'd need, for the press to dig up that I was in a 'cutest Cape lifeguards' book. Not the sort of thing I want to be known for."

I laugh. "I wouldn't worry. They'll probably never get it published."

"Oh, no," Rob says. "They'll do it. Those girls are *on it*. They're not playing." He shakes his head like he's scared.

I laugh. Then I remember what I need to do today. "I wish I could talk with Mum," I say. "She always has the best advice."

"Then do it," Rob says. "Here, take my phone." He flips open the cover of his slim silver cell phone, scrolls till he finds the number. "Take it up away from the waves where it's quiet and give her a call."

"Oh, my gosh, Rob. Thank you!" I hug him quickly. I'll be right back.

I run past the wide-eyed stares and gaping mouths of Tina and Ruby. "Careful, Ruby," I say, "you might swallow a fly."

I take the phone into one of the shower stalls. Too early in the day for anyone to be showering. I call Mum. She answers.

"Willa, honey! Oh, dear Lord. How are you? Riley! It's Willa! How are you, little sister? Oh, it's so good to hear your voice. . . ."

I can almost feel the hug from Mum's big, pillowy, soft arms.

"Oh, Mum . . ." I gush it all out, telling her about Will showing up, and him believing our birthfather was still alive, and how I have to break the awful news to him this morning, and how I just can't, just can't crush his dream like that. And what am I going to say to him?

"Willa?" Mum says.

"Yes."

"'The truth shall set you free.' John eight, verse thirty-two."

The truth shall set you free. I let those simple words sink into my spin-cycle self until I am soothed still.

"That's the wisest line in the Bible," Mum says. "Live by it, Willa, and I promise you . . . you'll save yourself a whole world of worrying."

"Thank you, Mum. I love you."

"Love you, too, baby. Now get to it."

I run back down to the beach to return Rob's phone to him. Tina and Ruby are on the case, both in full flirt mode, but Rob's not giving in.

He smiles a big, warm smile when he sees me. "Hey, Willa," he calls.

I hold up his phone; he reaches down to get it. "Thanks so much," I say.

"Anytime," he says. "Were you able to reach her?"

"Yes," I say. "And as always her advice was perfect."

"Good, I'm glad."

"Maybe you'd like to come to BUC with our family on Sunday? Bramble United Community church on Main Street. That's where Mum was the minister. The board is still searching for a replacement. That may take forever. There's nobody like Mum. But my stepfather, Sam, is filling in this summer."

"I'd like that," Rob says. "Thank you."

I tell him what time to meet us, and I'm off. "Watch those flies, Ruby!" I say, unable to resist.

I bike as fast as I can to Popponesset Beach and walk out to the Spit.

Will is tossing a stick into the water. Salty Dog runs to fetch it. Neither sees me yet. I stand there for a moment looking at my brother. Looking at my dog. All my life, I never had either. Then all at once for one short, sweet time, I had both.

When I tell Will the news, he'll leave Cape Cod and Salty will, too. *Poof.*

"I've got something to tell you, Will," I say.

He looks at my face, blue eyes to blue eyes. "And it isn't good. I can tell," he says.

I break the news as gently as possible.

Will's lips clench tight and he sniffs, turning his head away from me.

"No," he says. "Maybe he survived somehow. Maybe . . ."

"No, Will. I'm sorry. The coast guard report was final. He was declared dead on—"

Will raises his hand as if to say "Stop."

I do. I zip my lips. There's no need for words now.

"I want to be alone," Will says.

"Sure, I understand," I say.

I don't slap my leg. I don't say, "Come on, boy" to try to get Salty to follow. Will needs our dog right now. He needs him more than ever.

CHAPTER 22

Songs

Nothing can bring you peace but yourself.
—Ralph Waldo Emerson

Biking home, I feel lighter. Relieved of the burden of worrying. Mum's advice was perfect as always. I told the truth and now I am free.

At home in my room I call JFK. No answer. I leave another happy birthday message. "Call me."

I head into town to give Nana the CHANGE FOR GOOD ✪ jug I made for her.

"What a great idea," she says. "I'll put this right in my kitchen tonight."

"I'd like one, too," Dr. Swaminathan says to me when Nana turns to help a customer. "And if you could spare another, I have a friend who I think would appreciate one as well."

"Sure, Dr. S.," I say. "I'll make one for Mrs. Saperstone, too."

Dr. Swammy smiles. He puts his finger to his lips like, "Don't say anything to anybody."

I walk closer toward him. "Don't worry," I say. "Your secret's safe with me. But if you decide to pop the question, I know a good wedding planner."

Back home I seek out my mother. She's in the kitchen going over the schedule with the staff. I hand her the jug and tell her about Change For Good.

"Now that's a *big* idea, my daughter." She winks at me and smiles. We both know she's talking about my birthfather's company, What's the Big Idea?

Rosie asks if I'll make her a jug. Makita, Darryl, Mae-Alice . . . several of our staff members want one.

Mother follows me out of the kitchen. "Did you tell Will yet?" she says.

I nod my head yes. "I feel so bad for him," I say. "He really thought our father was alive."

"Poor kid," Mother says. "What a heartbreaking disappointment." She clears her throat. "Would you take me to meet him?"

"Sure," I say. "When?"

"I have a rehearsal tonight," Mom says. "But the

wedding isn't until six tomorrow night. Maybe we could go in the morning?"

"Sure, Mom."

It's Friday night and I have no plans. Chandler invited me over. Shefali and Caroline are coming to her house to plan out the sand castle they're going to build in the competition tomorrow. It sounds like fun, but I say thanks anyway, I have plans with my family. Maybe I'll see them tomorrow.

I check my messages. No reply from JFK.

Now I'm starting to get angry. I know it's his birthday, but he could at least answer my calls. He's probably having such a good time with that Lorna Doone girl and all those new rich friends at his grandparents' club that he — *Ring*. I jump.

I check caller ID. It's him!

Ring . . .

Don't act all desperate, Willa, like you've been waiting by the phone all day. Make him wonder a bit.

Ring . . .

Reason: It's JFK, Willa. Your boyfriend. You have been waiting for him to call. Answer it quick before . . .

Ring . . .

"Hello?" I say casually, like I don't know who's on the other end.

"Willa. It's me, Joseph."

"Oh, hi, Joseph."

"What's wrong?" he says.

"Nothing."

"Yes," he says. "Something's wrong. I can tell. You sound mad."

"No, I'm not mad."

Long pause.

"Happy birthday," I say.

"It would be if you were here," he says.

"What?" I heard him, but I want to hear it again.

"I said it would be a happy birthday if you were here."

My heart melts. "I miss you."

"I miss you, too," he says. "So much that I spent the whole day writing a song for you."

"For me?"

"Who else?" he says with a laugh.

"Really? You wrote me a song? What's it called?"

"'My Girl,'" he says.

"Sing it to me," I say.

"No way," he says. "I'm a lyricist, not a singer."

"Oh, come on, please."

"No. But you'll hear it soon enough. One of the kids down here for the summer, a grandson of one of my grandparents' best friends, is a DJ and an aspiring hip-hop artist. He made it through a few rounds of *American Idol* auditions."

"Wow," I say, "he must be good."

"He is," JFK says. "And I asked him to record my song for you."

Pause. My heart's a net full of butterflies fluttering.

"Willa," JFK says. "Did you hear me?"

"Yes," I say. "I'm speechless."

"You? Speechless? I don't think so!" We laugh.

"So who's this Lorna girl," I say.

JFK bursts out laughing. "There you go. I was wondering how long it would take for you to say something." He laughs and laughs and laughs.

"What does she look like?" I say.

"Oh, my God," he says, "she's gorgeous."

"What?"

"Just kidding. I don't know what she looks like. I don't really pay attention."

"I miss you," I say.

"Miss you more," he says.

"You wrote me a song?" I say. "That's the sweetest thing anyone's ever done for me. I can't wait to hear it."

"Well, right now I'm waiting for *my song*," JFK says.

"What song?" I say.

Pause. He laughs. "Did you forget? It's my birthday."

"Okay, okay," I say. "But don't laugh, because I'm no singer, either. All right, here goes:

Happy birthday to you,

Happy birthday to you,

Happy birthday, dear Jo . . . seph,

Happy birthday to you."

CHAPTER 23

Welcome Home

✶ ✶ ✶

To see a world in a grain of sand
And a heaven in a wild flower,
Hold infinity in the palm of your hand
And eternity in an hour.
— William Blake

When Mom and I get to the top of the beach stairs the next morning, we pause for a moment to take it all in. The waves, the sky, the birds, the beach, the cinnamon-sweet smell of the wild rugosa beach roses.

"Beautiful," Mother says.

"Sure is. Have you ever seen the sunrise here?"

"Not in a long, long time," Mom says. "I used to when I was younger, but no, not since I moved back here to the Cape."

"You'll have to come with me some morning," I say.

"I'd like that," Mom says.

"There's Will's boat," I say, nodding up toward the Spit.

We start down the beach stairs.

"What was that?" Mother says, pointing at the water. "A seal, maybe?"

We pause and look together for a while, but we don't see anything.

As we walk up the beach I tell her about the little girl who thought she saw a mermaid. "She was so certain of it," I say.

I remember how JFK thought the girl was silly but Will said, "What's off with you? You don't believe in mermaids?"

Poor Will. Here he came all this way to meet me. To find our father. He really believed Billy Havisham was still alive.

When we reach the tip of the Spit, Will is coming up over the bank, trudging through the sea grass with Salty Dog. Salty barks.

"Oh, my gosh, there's your dog," Mom says.

"Will's dog," I whisper, my heart clenching sadly.

When Mom sees Will's face, she raises her hand to her mouth.

I introduce them, but of course, no introductions are necessary.

Will holds out his hand.

Mother takes his hand between both of hers. She stares at him. "You're the spitting image of your father."

"Yeah," Will says with a weak smile. "So I understand."

"I'm so sorry you didn't know—" Mother starts.

"It's okay," Will interrupts, shaking his head. "I guess I really did know. I just didn't want to believe it."

We all stand there not saying anything for a few moments. Salty barks.

"How long are you staying on the Cape?" Mom asks.

"I'm leaving tomorrow."

"*What?*" I say. We only just met. "Tomorrow? Why so soon?"

"Nothing here for me now," Will says.

"What about *me?*" I blurt out, surprising myself.

Mother swings to look at me, equally surprised by my outburst.

"We only just met each other, Will," I say. "All this time I never realized I had a brother, and now you're leaving before we really even get to know each other?" I feel my body starting to shake, tears rising.

"Whoa," Will says. "I'm sorry, Willa. I didn't mean to hurt you."

"Do you have to leave tomorrow?" Mother says. "Is there any way we could talk you into staying with us for a while? We have room at the inn and we can always use an extra set of hands."

I burst out crying. That was the most spontaneous, most generous thing my mother has ever done. "Really, Mom? Do you mean it?"

"Of course," she says. "I need to check with Sam, but I'm sure he'd be on board."

"Will you, Will?" I say. "Will you stay?"

Ruff, ruff, ruff. Salty Dog licks Will's hand. He licks my hand. I swear that dog understands what's going on here.

"Sure," Will says. "I'm in no hurry to get back to the castle. No one's missing me there. Thanks for the offer. That would be nice."

* * *

Will rides over to the Vineyard to get his belongings. He'll meet us at the inn in a few hours.

Back at the Bramblebriar, Mom goes to talk with Sam in private. A few minutes later they are setting up a bed in the room that was going to be the nursery for the baby.

Mom asks Mae-Alice to put a brown comforter and dark blue pillows on the bed. "Make it as boyish as possible," she says.

Sam wheels in a television and a small refrigerator.

"Why don't you stock it with some juice and snacks," he says to me.

In the kitchen, I tell Rosie the news. "Oh, how wonderful!" she says. "Tell your mom and dad I want to make a special dinner just for the four of you. I'll serve it out in the Labyrinth like the other night."

✳   ✳   ✳

When Will shows up with Salty Dog, we're waiting for them on the porch.

Salty runs to me and I hug him. "Welcome home," I say.

Will looks at me, at Mom, at Sam. He looks like he's going to cry.

"Welcome to the Bramblebriar Inn," Sam says, reaching out his hand to shake my brother's.

"Welcome home," I say. I look quickly at my mother, then back at Will. "Well, at least for the summer," I say.

I reach down and bury my face in Salty's fur. "Furry traitor. I missed you, boy."

Salty licks my face. He licks my tears away. I laugh and he smiles at me.

Really, he does. The only dog I know that smiles.

"Let's get you settled," Sam says to Will. And we all head inside.

CHAPTER 24

Sand Castles, Sand Castles

Go and catch a falling star,
Get with child a mandrake root,
Tell me where all past years are, . . .
Teach me to hear mermaids singing.

— John Donne

Rosie has just finished baking the layers for the wedding cake for the couple from upstate New York. Denise and Scott. I put in the charms: B for book, R for rose, each letter standing for something special about our inn, "BRAMBLEBRIAR."

Tonight twelve guests will find a lucky penny under their plates and they'll be invited to pull a ribbon from the wedding cake. There will be a charm on the end of each ribbon. Hopefully the guests will assign a certain meaning to their charm . . . something that inspires them, or makes them feel good.

The charms were my idea. It's one of the things that makes a wedding at the Bramblebriar different from any other.

Sam finds a usable bike in the barn for Will, and the two of us bike over to South Cape Beach to check out the sand castle competition.

Sand creations, they should call them. People brought props and elaborate imaginations. Sand turtles, elephants, lizards, and dinosaurs. Villages, pyramids. Cartoon characters. Funny-shaped people of every sort. Hardly a traditional-shaped castle anywhere. The mermaids won't get many wedding cakes tonight.

It's late. We missed the announcement of the winners. But from the blue, red, and yellow banners by three amazing entries, Will and I can surmise who the first-, second-, and third-place winners were. Chandler and my friends from school took second place with a Dr. Seuss theme.

It's four-thirty or so. Families are packing up to head home for the day.

The roar of the ocean is picking up.

"Tide's coming in," Will says.

"Hey," I say. "Want to make a sand castle?"

"No," Will says. "Not really."

"Come on," I say. "It'll be fun. If we'd known each other when we were little, we'd have made tons of castles together."

Will smiles. "Sure. Okay. You're on."

We make a good old-fashioned sand castle. I make funny-looking gargoyles on the turrets. Will makes a moat. The waves fill it in with water.

"Do you have a moat at your castle in England?" I say.

Will laughs. "No, but we've got gargoyles."

We sit on the bank and look out at the water.

"Tide's coming in," Will says.

We look at our castle. Won't be long and it will be gone.

"Do you really think that little tourist girl saw a mermaid?" I ask.

"Of course she did," Will says without hesitation.

I look at him. "*What?* You really believe in mermaids?"

"Doesn't matter what I believe," Will says. "Who am I to say what she saw with her eyes?"

"But, Will, come on. A mermaid?"

He looks at me. "Tell me something."

"Sure, what?"

"If, two weeks ago, somebody told you that you have a brother, would you have believed them?"

I think about that. "No. I wouldn't have."

Will stares into my eyes. "Do you believe it now?"

"Of course. You're here. Right in front of me. I can see you with my own two eyes."

Waves are rolling in good now. There's a splash out on the water. A few drops spray across my face.

I look quick. Was that a tail? "Did you see that?" I say.

"No," my brother says. "But you did. And that's all that matters."

CHAPTER 25

Change For Good

Eat Taffy. Be Happy.

— Willa Havisham

The old wooden pews of Bramble United Community are full this Sunday morning. Sam, in his best gray suit, is standing up at the pulpit.

"We have some new faces at BUC this morning," Sam says. "New friends to welcome into our circle."

Sam looks at me and smiles. "Willa, will you do the honors?"

"Sure, Dad." I stand and face the congregation. "Please join me in welcoming my brother, Will Havisham, visiting us this summer from England."

Will stands and waves and sits back down. There's a twittering throughout the room and then several "welcomes," "glad to meet you's," and "so happy you could join us."

"And," I say, smiling at Rob to let him know he's next up, "I'd like to introduce Rob Whitebridge, on summer break from Boston College, nephew of our own dear friend and former minister, Sulamina Mum."

There are gasps and then applause. Rob stands and nods his gratitude.

"Geesh," Rob whispers to me. "I don't have to give a speech or anything, do I?"

"No," I whisper back. "But I can tell you right now, some of these ladies are going to want your autograph."

Rob bursts out laughing.

My mother gives me the "quiet down" look.

There are announcements and a reading. The choir sings "Let It Be a Dance," a song about how to live your life freely with a joyful heart.

Sam takes the pulpit for the sermon.

"I must admit I'm a little nervous," he says, "even having a *relative* of Sulamina Mum's in the building."

There's a light wave of laughter across the room.

"But I know Mum, our for-a-time minister and forever friend, would approve of the topic I've chosen for today's sermon. That topic is service. Community rent. How you and I and each of us can make a difference with our one small life."

Sam talks on and on. I look at my mother's face, so happy, so proud.

I look at Rob's face, smiling, glad to be here.

I look at my brother's face.

Will senses me staring at him and turns to wink at me.

I look behind me at Nana. She nods toward Will and Rob and gives me a thumbs-up sign.

I look back at Mrs. Saperstone and Dr. Swaminathan. Mrs. Saperstone smiles at me and leans her head in toward Dr. Swammy's shoulder.

I look two rows over at the Sivlers and the Belles. Tina and Ruby are sitting together and yet I'm not jealous. That is how it should be.

I think of JFK and Mariel, wishing they both were here.

"And so," Sam says, "I hope I won't embarrass my stepdaughter, Willa, by telling all of you about her wonderful, simple idea called Change For Good."

✸ ✸ ✸

It's late and I'm exhausted. I open up a new skinny-punch. *Feathers* by Jacqueline Woodson. One of my favorite authors.

Before the story starts there is a quote from Emily Dickinson, one of my other all-time favorite authors.

Hope is the thing with feathers
that perches in the soul,
And sings the tune—without the words,
And never stops at all.

✳ ✳ ✳

I pull on a sweatshirt and head up to the widow's walk.

The air is cool, refreshing. The sky takes my breath away.

I wish I may, I wish I might, have the wish I wish tonight.

I stare out at the vast, dark ocean, thinking briefly of mermaids.

"Hope you liked the sand castle Will and I sent you yesterday. Hope it turned into a beautiful wedding cake. Hope it was delicious."

I close my eyes and smile.

I breathe in and out.

Thank you.

Two simple words.

Mum always said that was the best prayer.

Thank you.

Thank you for my life. My mom. My dad. My dog. My house. My Nana. JFK. Mariel and all my friends. My town. My books. My *brother*.

Thank you.

That's all.

Thank you.

I turn and head in, and as I do I hear singing somewhere off at sea.

"Good night," I call out with a laugh. "Sleep tight. Oh, and . . . a dog? A brother? *Really cool gifts.* Keep 'em coming. Surprise me. Summer's only just begun."

Willa's Summer Skinny-Punch Pix List #2

Feathers, Jacqueline Woodson
42 Miles, Tracie Vaughn Zimmer
The Pearl, John Steinbeck
Skellig, David Almond
Song of the Trees, Mildred D. Taylor
The House on Mango Street, Sandra Cisneros
The Little Prince, Antoine de Saint-Exupéry
Three Cups of Tea (Young Reader's Edition), Greg
    Mortenson and David Oliver Relin
Tuck Everlasting, Natalie Babbitt
Yellow Star, Jennifer Roy

Dear Reader,
    What are some of your favorite books? Maybe you'd like to make your own Pix List.

                  Happy Reading,
                  ⭐ *Coleen*

_____ 's

Pix List

_____

_____

_____

_____

_____

_____

_____

_____

_____

Acknowledgments

With sincerest appreciation to:

My mother, Peg Spain Murtagh, my anchor.

My wonderful editor, Jennifer Rees, and David Levithan, Lillie Mear, and all of Willa's friends at Scholastic Press and Scholastic Book Clubs and Fairs.

My Cape Cod friends: Bill Malone, Claire and Chris Kondochristie, Rowena Lammer, Gail and Joe DeBattista, Fran and Rick Risko, Doris O'Neil, Cookie and Don McGinness, Ray and Lynn Butti, Judy and Steve LeGraw, Betty Stefos, Jan and Joe Bosse, Wendy and John Alexopolus, Nancy and Bobby Farrelly, Paul Rifkin, Annie Lawrence, Janet Burke, Sara Young, Tara Nickerson, Karen Beil, Lisa Trepanier, Joanne Doggart, Sybille Colby, Debbie Dermady, and especially Carol Chittenden, in celebration of the legions of readers and writers she has nurtured and inspired through her wonderful Eight Cousins bookstore, Falmouth, Cape Cod.

My dear friends Pauline and Fred Miller, who, when I was in a panic over losing a computer file with nearly two-thirds of this manuscript completed, kept cool and kept on believing and all around saved the day.

My Ya-Ya's: Ellen Donovan, Paula Davenport, and Kathy Johnson.

Selwyn, for the song.

My writing buddies: Robyn Ryan, Ellen Laird, Karen Beil, Kathleen Elkin, Nancy Castaldo, Rose Kent, Eric Luper, Kyra Teis, Liza Frenette, Lois Feister Huey, Jennifer Groff, Debbi Mickho Florence, Jackie Rogers, Peter Marino, Peter DeWitt, and Robert Whiteman.

My colleagues in the Children's Literature Connection and the Upstate New York chapter of SCBWI (Society of Children's Book Writers and Illustrators).

My wonderful family, especially my sons, Connor, Dylan, and Christopher, once super sand castle builders, now building fine lives for themselves. You make me so proud.

And, finally, to my readers . . . May you always have good books and sweet treats on your nightstand and a heart wide open to the gifts of the sea.

Splash, splash, surprise!

Till soon,
✪ *Coleen*